MW01488776

Max Unlocks
the Universe

Max Unlocks
the Universe

Mark Bouton

Five Star • Waterville, Maine

This novel is a work of fiction. Names, characters, places and incidents are either the product of the author's imagination, or, if real, used fictitiously.

First Edition
First Printing: September 2006

Published in 2006 in conjunction with Tekno Books and Ed Gorman.

Set in 11 pt. Plantin.

Printed in the United States on permanent paper.

Library of Congress Cataloging-in-Publication Data

Bouton, Mark.
    Max unlocks the universe / Mark Bouton.—1st ed.
        p. cm.
    ISBN 1-59414-488-5 (hc : alk. paper)
    1. Private investigators—Fiction.   2. Computer scientists—Crimes against—Fiction.   I. Title.
    PS3602.O894M394 2006
    813'.6—dc22   2006008488

This book is dedicated to my wife,
Ellen Byers Bouton,
who has always encouraged and supported me
in my writing and in life.

Acknowledgement

Many thanks go out to those who have helped with this book, including John Helfers, Acquisitions Editor, and Pat Estrada, editor at Tekno Books; Mary P. Smith, Managing Editor, and Tiffany Schofield, Acquisitions Editor at Five Star Publishing; Nancy Ellis, my agent; and Milton Kahn, my publicist. I'm also grateful for the support from my writers' groups: The Kansas Author's Club; Kansas Fiction Writers, Inc.; the Pike's Peak Writer's Club; Sisters in Crime; and the Mystery Writers of America. And many thanks to the fine men and women of the FBI and other law enforcement groups throughout the country who serve as inspiration for my fictional tales.

Chapter 1

"Place looks like it got nuked," says Bones.

Carl squints, his brow scrunched up like a bulldog's. "Whadduya mean?"

"Like when an H-bomb explodes?" He jerks a thumb at the furious snowstorm. "You get nuclear winter—just like this crap."

Carl nods, silent as a sphinx.

"When you think it'll stop, Carl?"

The wipers clatter across the windshield, leaving a trail. Carl grins. "Prob'ly about June."

"You're such a riot." *And a Neanderthal—hulking shoulders, hairy hands on the wheel, shaved head shining like a Cadillac hubcap.*

Sighing, Bones flips on the defroster, then pulls a rag from his pocket and attacks the windshield, making urgent mouse squeaks. *Jeez, still can't see jack. Stupid storm—makes it hard to waste someone.* A pause, then he chuckles.

"What's so funny?" Carl says, caressing his smooth dome.

"Nothing," he says, his mind moving on: *Pistol's poking my ribs, my back aches, I gotta pee like a racehorse. What next?*

Carl thrums his fingers on the wheel. Whistles an aimless tune. Gazes across the street. Then he turns his head, his neck cracking like a dry branch. "Next time it might be in Florida, huh? Don't matter that it's January, there's still lots of sun, women—all that good stuff."

"Bring it on, man, the Midwest bites." He makes a face, thinking, *Just like this job. But what can I do? They've got me by the balls.*

Carl growls, "Um hmm." Then he smacks the wheel. "Where *is* the guy?"

Bones aims his binoculars. "He's gotta come out soon, they've all left but two."

"Hell, it's gonna get dark. Anyway, I'm cranked to get outta here."

"Damn straight." He reaches for the heater lever, muttering, "Jeez, I'm freezing my . . . oh, hey, look!" He trains the glasses on two figures emerging from the house. "Just could be."

The young men trudge a few feet and stop. They're yakking, ignoring the storm. One's slender, wearing a neon-blue coat, the other one husky, all in black. Bones pulls a photo from his coveralls, glances at the stamp of a woman's head on the back, then checks the image.

"So, give," Carl says.

Bones angles the photo toward him. "What do you think?"

"The skinny one?"

"He's just slim, Carl. Anyway, you're damn right—it's showtime."

Bones opens a cooler on the floorboard and extracts a dart, being careful of the tip.

"They're moving," says Carl.

Bones looks up. They're tramping across the yard, ankle-deep in drifts, heading for a Porsche in the driveway. He loads the pistol.

They stop beside the car. The lanky one pulls open the door, grabs a scraper, and skins packed snow off the back window. Then he moves forward to the windshield.

No traffic, and no one outside. Good as it'll get. "Keep the motor running, Carl."

Out of the van, Bones slogs down the sidewalk, the wind an icy knife slicing his face. The one in blue is facing him, so Bones keeps moving. When he's past the young men, he cuts across the street, moving like a hunter tracking a deer. Merging with the blowing flakes, he stops beside the curb, hidden from view by a pear-shaped evergreen. He judges the distance to his target.

Blue Jacket tosses the scraper back into the Porsche. Now he turns his back, seeming to be arguing with the stout one. They're both waving their arms, looking agitated.

Bones raises the pistol, then pauses. *The jacket's a problem. With the car in the way, that just leaves a head shot.* He sights in, then tightens on . . . but now the guy leans down to flick ice off the outside mirror.

Finger on the trigger, Bones waits until the young man straightens, then he looks left and right down the street. *Nothing.* He takes aim . . . *steady, steady* . . . then pulls the trigger.

Keening wind masks the sound. The dart stabs the young man's neck, he stiffens, then slumps forward against the door frame and crumples to the ground. Retreating to the van, Bones yanks open the door and clambers in.

"Good shot," says Carl.

"Shut up. Let's go."

Carl hits the accelerator, the van speeds up, and they vanish into a white veil of obscurity.

Wheeling my Trailblazer through the storm, the light fading, I think I'm crazy to be out here, because four-wheel drive or no, the Chevy's lurching and sliding, making my heart clutch like a fist and the hair go electric on my neck. But when Detective Bagley said, "Max, it's urgent," his voice pinched and tinny over the line, I told him I was on my way. I'd never question the man who once saved my life.

Slowing, I enter the clogged street: patrol units, an EMT van, detectives' cars—their harsh lights barely piercing the whiteout conditions. I skid to a stop, slap on my ball cap and step out into the arctic commotion. Spotting Bagley, I tramp over to him, and say, "So, what's the story?"

Bagley frowns. "My son's in trouble, Max. Let's talk in my car."

I limp to his sedan, the cold, wet weather making my bad leg ache. Once we're closed in with the smell of wet coats, holster leather, and cigar smoke, Bagley sags into his seat, saying, "It looks real bad, Max. I hope you can . . ." His usually commanding voice goes hoarse; his forceful bulk seems to shrink.

"What's the problem, Jeff? Something about David?"

Bagley looks toward the yard bordered by yellow tape. "Kyle Mossler got killed. They think David did it."

That's totally weird. Jeff's son is a fine young man and a computer whiz who runs his own company. "There was an accident? They think David was involved?"

He hesitates. "They believe Mossler was murdered. And that David killed him."

For a moment, I just stare at him. "That's insane. David's a great kid."

"I know, but I can't work it. Could you take a look around, see what you think?"

"Is it okay with the chief?" Hillsboro's a small town; the top cop likes to keep control.

"He said he'd let you consult."

I slap the legs of my jeans. "Then why are we sitting here?"

★ ★ ★ ★ ★

The corpse is lying next to a new, fire-colored Porsche, a fancy ride for northeast Kansas.

"It's Mossler's car," Bagley says, apparently reading my mind.

Hal Owen, another detective, walks up. "Hey, Max Austin. I heard you were coming. Gonna lend us your FBI expertise?"

Hal knows I've been a private eye since my car wreck two years ago—he's just pulling my chain. But two can play this game. "Hal, I thought you clue hounds already had it solved."

He glances at Bagley, a gray look on his face, then turns back to me. "Nah, we're still checking stuff out."

I mentally kick myself. *Already have it solved.* Sure, David's in cuffs, and I'm a fool.

As Owen walks off, I say, "Sorry for that dumb remark, Jeff. My mouth can be bigger than both my feet."

He shrugs. "Guess you've had your head in the stars too long. You're just screwed up from all that astronomy shit."

"Maybe staring at so much space warped my brain."

"So when you get back to Earth, could you get busy on this?"

"You got it. What's the theory here?"

"Kyle Mossler was in David's software company," he says, "together with four other kids." He pauses and clears a catch in his throat. "They had a meeting this afternoon. When it broke up, David left the house with Kyle."

"Um hmm."

"They were talking beside the car, and Mossler just dropped in the snow. By the time the EMTs got here, he was dead."

This seems like that Rubik's Cube where the colorful

11

pieces don't match up, at least not for me. "I don't get it. What am I missing?"

"You know, Mossler was a track star at KU."

I don't follow sports. "Sure."

"He still kept in shape—running, cycling."

"Then how'd he die, drugs?"

"David swears none of them uses. Tests will tell, of course."

"What do you think *did* happen?"

"David told me Mossler fainted and hit his throat on the frame of the car door. EMTs called it . . ." Bagley pauses to touch his throat. ". . . a 'collapsed larynx.' Basically, he couldn't breathe. He died of asphyxiation."

I'm feeling dizzy myself. I need to examine the body and talk to the other cops, but first I ask, "So why'd they point the finger at David?"

Bagley stares at the footprints in the snow, as if they'll tell him some secret. "The Sanders kid lives here. He looked out the window and saw David and Kyle arguing. They'd gotten into it at the meeting, too. He saw David's arm lash out toward Mossler just before he dropped."

Ah, now I'm getting it. David is a big guy, like his dad, but he didn't play hoops or football, he pumped iron and took karate. "They think David hit him?"

"Healthy kids don't just drop dead."

"But can't the ME tell the difference by the injury?"

"I'm praying he can."

Sometimes the police jump to conclusions and arrest folks before they've proved a case. And the influence of big bucks could be having an effect. "Tell me about the other young men."

"Most are computer nerds. A couple are engineers, one a mathematician. They sell software programs. Advertise on the Net. All that gobbledy gook."

So, I'm in alien territory. "These others see anything?"

"They left before the incident," Bagley says. "Three are from out-of-state: Texas, California, and Colorado. They're staying at a motel, and our guys are on the way there."

"Theories are cheap, Jeff. And asteroids, like Toutatis, pass by us all the time, but unless one strikes the Earth, no harm, no foul. Don't worry, I'll pull David out of this crazy black hole."

"Max, that would mean . . ." He sniffs, then slugs me with a short left jab to the shoulder, rattling my teeth. "I knew I could count on the 'Conqueror of the Cosmos.' "

Some of the cops started calling me that after we solved the mob hit a few months ago. It's a nickname I can live without. So I merely nod, but I realize this is like navigating a new galaxy; you never know what you might slam into.

A buzz saw wakes me from my nighttime slumbers. No, I recognize as my head clears a bit, it's just Binga, my adenoidal German shepherd, collapsed in the corner like a pile of old tires. I peer outside at sunslants glancing off frosted fields, and I'm dazzled by the brash beauty of the hilly wonderland capped with a half foot of puffy whiteness.

I rouse the old gal from her comatose state, and we head downstairs for breakfast. "Jeff's son is in big trouble," I say. Binga cocks her head, listening. She seems saddened by the news, but not enough to stop her ravenous attack on the bowl of crunchies I set on the floor. Absently, I munch on a bagel and sip some milk.

I'm preoccupied about last night's killing, or sudden accidental death, or whatever it was. But I need to read the police reports to store details in my head. Bagley said they wouldn't be ready until ten this morning, which is more than two hours away.

Stepping onto the porch, I decide I need a distraction. Maybe some exercise . . . aha, perhaps I'll go conquer those slopes. Binga's busy making yellow snow, but when she finishes, I whistle, getting her wary attention.

With a sledding disk tucked under my arm, I trek across the yard toward my huge red barn. Binga limps along a few paces behind. She's panting, clearly the martyr.

A red-tailed hawk screeches high above us, cutting a languid arc in the blue. I watch as it glides on the updrafts, its keen gaze intent for signs of movement below. Does he have a mate, I wonder, with whom to share the spoils of the hunt? To tell of his conquests? Maybe she's even sympathetic about his failures.

I miss such intimacy with Sharon; it's hard to fathom that she's gone. Ovarian cancer, the doctor told us, matter-of-factly, more than a year ago. Twenty-five years of marriage, two children.

Life goes on, they say, but what of the quality? Some spark is missing. There's a black hole in my personal universe.

We reach the large knoll behind my barn. A thick stand of cedars, walnuts, and elms borders the west, and to the north and east there's a panoramic vista of farmland and fields. Houses, barns, and water towers punctuate the view for miles.

I locate a prime launching spot—a slope that drops thirty feet at a moderate rate. With enthusiasm, I try to coax Binga aboard the disk, but she regards me with haunted brown eyes that say: Please, I no longer do such things. So, alone, I accept the challenge.

After several attempts at the world land speed record on a fifty-meter run, I'm gulping like a landlocked fish. I decide one more foray should be plenty. I make a face at Binga, the sissy, then fold my legs like a contortionist and push off, plummeting downward at warp speed.

Within moments I crash and sprawl in an unrefined pose in a tricky snowdrift. Brushing white stuff and twigs off my coat, I hobble up the hill while Binga studies my awkward labors. I swear she rolled her eyes, the cur.

"Race you back to the house," I say, and we tramp through the downy blanket. Air escapes my lungs in visible clouds. The evergreens, laden and drooping, look like portly polar bears. To avoid comparison, I suck in my gut. Best lose that ten before the Olympics.

Back on the porch, I grab a broom and sweep off my boots. Binga paces, eager to enter the warm abode and flop on her cushiony mat. We call the race a draw, but I'm pretty sure I won.

Inside, I grab a dog biscuit and a Diet Coke and head for the living room. Binga pads ahead of me, then whirls and stares intently, moaning in human-sounding tones, obviously fixed on the morsel in my hand. "Okay, girl," I say, "let's see Circus Dog."

When she was younger, she'd balance on her haunches until I tossed the biscuit, then hop and snare it in mid-air. But arthritis has stiffened her hips, and now she just leans back into a crouching position, then when the biscuit's airborne, she lunges to grab it, pretending she's soared off the floor. Hey, we all fool ourselves about our abilities, especially as we lose them.

I go back to the kitchen to get some pills which help to make her more limber. I stick them inside a ball of raw hamburger. And she eagerly swallows them down.

Glancing at my telescope sitting in the bay window, I sigh, thinking I won't be using it for a while, then I ensconce myself in my mocha-colored leather chair, feet on the ottoman, to consider the crime. Concentration summons the power of the

Cosmos, which I may need here. Together with a positive attitude.

In my mind's eye, I see the body slumped on the ground beside the open driver's door of Kyle Mossler's Porsche. Only David and Pete Sanders were at the scene. The neighbors who were contacted by the cops said they witnessed nothing.

I stare at Binga, sprawled in canine sanguinity on her mat in the corner, as I wonder what could have happened to that healthy kid to make him keel over dead as he was about to climb into his car. Nothing comes to mind, except that death is inevitable for everyone in this Homo sapiens soup. "I suppose it's just a matter of when your number comes up," I remark, then mentally kick myself for being so callous in the presence of an elderly canine.

Binga shifts on her mat, twitches her nose, but doesn't open her eyes. I think about the position of Mossler's body, what the EMTs said about his collapsed larynx and subsequent asphyxiation, and about the red mark found on his throat, indicating a recent blow. Sanders said David and Mossler had quarreled during the meeting, then David appeared to hit Mossler. Two sets of footprints in the snow tracked from the house to Mossler's car.

I can only surmise, as did the detectives, that the first set of footprints was made by Mossler walking from his vehicle to the house for the meeting, and back to the car afterwards. The second set of footprints (which will be confirmed by tests) was thought to be that of David walking out to the Porsche, then running back to the house.

Mossler parked his power ride in the driveway. David left his Mustang at the curb. The other kids at the meeting also parked in the driveway, then walked along the sidewalk leading to the front door. David and Mossler both wore boots, so they hoofed across the snowy lawn.

I worked a case in a small Kansas town where two young guys held up a bank president and his wife at their house, trying to force the man to return to the bank and open the vault. He convinced them it was on a time lock and he couldn't get in, so, instead, they tied the couple up and left with some cash and their car. But they left footprints in the snow. About a month later, when I interviewed a suspect, he crossed his foot atop his knee, unwittingly displaying the tread design I'd been seeking. Busted.

Criminals leave many kinds of tracks when they practice their nefarious craft. Why they never learn this amazes me. Since crime seldom pays, at least not in ways they expect (don't do the crime if you can't do the time), couldn't they learn welding or plumbing or roofing?

I suppose there's no thrill in those jobs, and you can't use drugs and lie in bed until noon. But then, you don't have to shower with huge, horny guys, either. Everything's a trade-off.

Back to this crime, if it was one—I'm anxious to see the coroner's report. The snow-covered ground where Mossler collapsed didn't look like the scene of a scuffle. Although if David did strike just a single, deadly blow, the contest would have been over in short order.

I'll go meet with Arty Carpenter and Hal Owen at the PD to get their take on the matter. Then I'll talk with David, who I'm sure can use some support. I'd especially like to know why he walked over to Mossler's Porsche right before the young man croaked.

I shower, shave, and don my working stiff attire: dark blue sports coat, jeans, and a light blue oxford cloth shirt. No tie. Black sneakers. I'm no longer a slave to bureaucratic dictates.

Firing up my Trailblazer, I carve tracks along the driveway, then turn onto the gravel road that fronts my property. The snow hasn't been cleared by a dozer, but ruts are grooved almost to the nubby surface; some of my neighbors must have left for their construction jobs, and their trucks plow through the snow well. Unfortunately, they drop lots of hazardous screws and nails.

Thirty minutes later, I pull up in front of the Hillsboro Police Station, a low beige-tinted building with dark green trim. I push through the glass doors, ask the receptionist for Arty Carpenter, and wait until he appears to let me into the sanctum sanctorum of crime-busting. We pace down the hallway to the squad room, which is abuzz with detectives doping out the whys and wherefores of the Kansas City Chiefs' latest contest.

"What's your take on the game?" tall Paul Sikes (six-foot-five and skinny as a coat rack) asks me when we stop on the fringe of the group. I hesitate, as I didn't see the game. Two beefy guys named Harmon and Jeter stare at me, an atavistic challenge in their eyes as they await my manly answer, while a trim female I haven't met before turns her starbright blue eyes upon me.

"I thought the penalties and turnovers really hurt them," I say. Safe conjecture, the Chiefs always have those problems. She's got a shine of smarts in those eyes that I really like.

"Shit, that damn interception at the start of the second half almost killed them," says Jeter.

"And the holding call on that pass play in the last minute nearly ate our lunch," Harmon adds.

"Yeah, those are the ones I meant," I say, nodding.

"I'm Paula Jackson," she says, holding out her hand. "I don't think we've met."

I tell her my name. Her grip is strong, her hand warm. She

may not be forty yet. Oh, well. Some lucky guy will meet her someday.

"But they'll probably still rumble through the playoffs," Arty observes. Then he motions for me to follow him to his cubicle. Owen joins us, and we all sit down and stare at each other.

Arty has a blank look on his placid face. He's mid-forties, with a full head of pecan-colored hair, and with greenish eyes that have seen a lot but still seem to believe in man's inherent goodness. That puts him in a minority among the detectives.

Owen's gaze from dark brown eyes, hooded with black, bushy eyebrows, is more intense, brooding. He's either always got a tan or there's a swarthy tint to his skin. Medium tall, he sports thick muscles and curling dark hair on his forearms.

I wait. They say nothing. "So what've you got on the kid?" I ask.

Arty winces. Owen grimaces. No one there wants Bagley's kid to be in trouble. Especially bad trouble like this. But we all have a job to do, and there you have it.

"Looks bad," Owen finally says in his deep, gravelly voice.

"You get the autopsy report?" I ask.

"Not yet," Arty says. "Maybe tomorrow."

"Might've been a simple accident," I say. "Or maybe a stroke?"

"But you've got the red mark on his throat," says Owen. "Collapsed larynx. Witness to a possible karate strike by David."

"Maybe he passed out," I say, "then fell on the car door frame, like David said."

"Healthy kid faints, just like that?" asks Arty.

I shrug. "He could've used drugs."

Owen palms his face. "Coroner's checking on that."

19

"It just seems there are lots of possibilities besides David hitting him, which he denies."

They glance at each other. Thinking, I'm sure, that every perp they've ever caught has always denied their crime. It's the outlaw code of self-preservation.

Owen says, "That'll be the coroner's call, too. Guess we'll know whether he did it or not when we get the autopsy report."

I hold out my hands in supplication. "Fellows, the eyewitness is indecisive. David says he didn't hit the boy. He's got no priors, and he's a good, clean kid. There's no sign of a struggle. No motive. No way to prove he hit Mossler. It's all circumstantial. And weak."

Arty won't meet my gaze. "Yeah, but . . ."

"What?"

"We're getting heat from the mayor's office. Some muckety-mucks in town are upset."

"Lady Justice wears a blindfold," I say. "She can't tell a perp in a tux from one in jeans."

Owen looks miffed. "So find us another karate expert, dress him however you want, and we'll cuff him and put him away."

"You know I'm just—"

"One thing, though," he cautions.

"What's that?"

"Better make sure he can fly. Our lab guy just confirmed Mossler's and David's footprints were the only ones going to that Porsche."

Chapter 2

On my way to the jail I pass the federal building, a four-story brick job where I used to work. Lots of memories there. Time spent searching for answers to the whys and wherefores of criminal activities. Sometimes finding them. Sometimes theorizing what could power the galaxy of crime, much the way scientists speculate that black holes energize our Universe.

I thought I'd finished with that battle, but somehow I keep getting pulled back into the fray, an attraction as ephemeral but ubiquitous as gravitational waves throughout the Universe. Am I only a moon or some other type of satellite that will forever orbit about the central body of crime and its practitioners? No, somehow I think this is different.

For one thing, I have a choice as to whether to work this matter. And for another, I'm seeking more to absolve the son of a friend than to find the true perpetrator, though the two pursuits will, in fact, be intertwined. Much like strands of DNA.

At the county jail I find a parking spot, kill the engine, and stare at the dark building which strikes me rather like a mausoleum, a place where all hope has been dashed. I limp to the doors and push my way in. At the reception desk sits Rosie, a hefty guard in a tight-to-bursting uniform. We exchange hellos and how you beens, then I ask to talk with David.

"You armed?" she asks.

"Left my assault rifle in my tank outside."

"Then you best use the door over there for smartasses."

I head for the only entrance, and she hits a button which retracts a thick bolt with a solid metallic thunk. Past that door, then another, I enter the stench of pine cleaner and fear. Eventually I find myself in a small Spartan room sitting in a chair perfectly designed to torture the human spine. In a few minutes, a guard brings David to the door.

He's dressed in a too-small orange jumpsuit, his hair askew, stubble on his chin. His eyes are cast downward, and he's as pale as skim milk. Looks to be in shock.

I stand up to shake his hand, which is damp. He's a stocky young man, tall, with light brown hair. Intense eyes peer from behind tortoiseshell glasses.

"How's it going, David?" I motion for him to sit, which he does.

"We had rubbery chicken and stale toast for lunch. And a couple of guys in there look like they want to stomp me. I'm not afraid of a fight, but I don't want to catch a shiv in the ribs."

"Whatever happened to mild-mannered thugs?"

He gives me a look.

"Just kidding. I know it's no party here, son."

"Can you get me out?"

"When's your hearing?"

"Three o'clock."

"Let's see how that goes. I don't think they'll have much choice but to let you out on bail. I'm more concerned about where it goes from there."

"Me, too, but mostly I want to bounce out of this hell-hole."

I nod. "Sure you do. But I need to find out what happened to Kyle. What can you tell me?" I take a notepad and a pen from my jacket pocket and lay them on the table between us.

"I'm not really sure, man. It happened so fast. I thought he fainted or something."

"He collapsed right in front of you?"

"Yeah, in fact, he was talking. He just stopped in the middle of a sentence, his eyes got big, and he grabbed at his neck."

"Then dropped to the ground?" I make some notes, but keep glancing at David's eyes. They're shifting to the right, remembering the scene, not making it up as he talks.

"He looked like a robot that froze up, then he stumbled forward a step, and I reached out to him, but he slumped to the ground. Like I told the cops, I think he hit his throat on the top of the door frame as he went down."

"Wasn't the door standing open as you two talked?"

He thinks about it. "He was about to get in, so the door was halfway open, between us."

Which makes the physics plausible. "What were you talking about?"

"We'd been arguing. But then I decided, what the heck. I apologized, saying we should just mindshare and drop the hassle."

"You mean work it out?"

"Close enough to be on the menu."

"Was he willing to try?"

"I don't know. He never finished what he was saying. And he . . ." He stares at the wall.

"He what?"

"Nothing. We just had different philosophies about computer use."

"Such as?"

"Is this important?"

"I'm not sure, but I like to know the background of what I'm investigating."

He looks doubtful, but there's a thump against a wall, and I can see visions of large, ugly inmates dancing in his head.

He sighs, then says, "Kyle was into cracking, phreaking, and snarfing, which a lot of techies are, but I'm not."

"Is cracking the same as hacking?"

"No, hacking is done by people who are computer savvy and like to see what they can access, testing their system's capabilities. Cracking means you're trying to steal information or screw up other people's programs or operating systems."

"Phreaking and snarfing about the same as cracking?"

"Yeah, sorta variations. You have people who use a computer for solving important problems and making living conditions better. Then you've got those that write Trojan horse programs, viruses, worms—anything to mess up what could be a worthwhile tool for us all."

"Was that what you and Kyle were arguing about?"

He leans forward and places his palms on the table. He has large hands, the kind that'd make a chop to the neck very effective. "This really has nothing to do with his death."

That remains to be seen. But I learned a little interview trick over the years that I call "water flows around a rock." If you can't get the answers you need by attacking the rock directly, you keep the questions flowing until you reconnect them on the other side.

"So what did you do after he fell down?"

He stares at those big hands. "I called out his name, then shook him, but he didn't answer. He just lay there, gulping like a fish."

"Did you give him mouth-to-mouth?"

"I'm not trained in CPR. But I felt his carotid artery, and his pulse seemed weak. Meatware is too damn transitory."

"Meatware?"

"The human body."

"Ahhh. So what'd you do next?"

"Ran back to the house and yelled at Pete to call 9-1-1."

"Which he did?"

"Must've. I went back out to see if Kyle had recovered. But, to tell the truth, I sorta froze up. I couldn't go back to him, I could only stare. And he never moved."

"Did the police get there soon?"

"Yeah, the cops, then an ambulance, both within a few minutes, I'd guess."

Four minutes after the call, in fact. "What was Kyle saying when he collapsed?"

David takes a deep breath, leans back against his chair, and folds his arms. Looking away from me he says, "I really don't remember."

I lay down my pen and study him, trying to get to the other side of this stubborn boulder.

His eyes flick back to mine, then he studies the tabletop. "I think he was going to crunch an idea for me. But, as I said, he was cut off."

I pick up my pen and tap it on the tabletop. "If the prosecutor tries to pin this on you, I think he'll make a lot out of your quarrel. I need to know about it."

He thinks about that, his lips clamped together. "All right," he says. "Kyle had done some serious tweaking on an algy we'd developed."

"An algy?"

"An algorithm. The rules you write to set up a computer program."

"You've lost me, David." Not completely, but I want to see where this goes.

"Call it magic. Too technical to describe."

"Give it a shot," I say, my face going rigid.

He looks troubled. "Okay, I'll try. Our company, Zipdata,

had written a security software program we were selling to companies. To diagram it for you user-friendly, Kyle had messed up the program, and I found out about it."

"What was he trying to do?"

"I'm not sure. We'd already sold this particular program to several corporations and a couple of government agencies. Maybe he wanted to steal some data."

"Was there anything unusual about the program?"

"You bet. We were using advanced encryption techniques. Kyle and Will Tanger, a guy from San Antonio, both specialize in them. They'd developed a new method, really cutting-edge stuff, which we put in the program."

I've read about encryption, but not enough to follow the scenario. "What was the program supposed to do?"

"Basically, it was a firewall setup, with encryption to protect both stored data and wireless command ports. And it had a foolproof method for detecting and stopping crackers. We figure we had everything blocked, from spyware to viruses to worms."

"But Kyle and Will could get in?"

He scrutinizes me. "You ask good questions. Yep, they'd put a Trojan horse into the program, and with that implanted, they could bypass the safeguards, gather whatever data they wanted, even block access to other programs. In effect, they could screw up the system, even make it inoperable if they wanted to."

"Did they want to?"

"I don't know." He shrugs, then says, "I doubt it, but why the hell did they do it?"

"Can you tell the cops about this?"

He grimaces. "I doubt that they'd understand the significance. Or even believe me. Besides these are confidential business ideas you're asking about."

I presume he doesn't want to discuss it anymore.

"Anything else I should know?"

"I really can't tell you anything else. Our ideas are the only valuable part of our company. You know, ninety-five percent of Internet companies are basically just new concepts—we're not dealing in brick-and-mortar factories turning out goods."

"Like Goodyear?" Which has a big tire factory in Hillsboro.

He rolls his eyes and nods.

"Then you're more ephemeral. Say, like the helium gas in the Goodyear blimp?"

He gives me a crooked smile. "That's our default mode."

So is what he's telling me so much hot air?

Chapter 3

Hunger pangs have struck, so I drive to Schlotzky's, a soup and sandwich spot that's presently thronged with men in dark suits, women wearing print dresses, and kids sporting the grunge de jour. Upstairs, tray in hand, I find a table by a window. Munching on a ham sandwich, I study people scurrying down the sidewalks. But mostly I'm contemplating David; I feel he's holding back on me, and I don't like the implications.

It could just be that he doesn't want to reveal his company's ideas, as he said, but I feel there's more to it. He was evasive about what he and Kyle Mossler were discussing prior to Mossler keeling over. And if David's not being forthcoming about that, he may be lying about not hitting Kyle, and about anything else.

Which pretty much gets down to the subatomic crux of this situation: whether David hit Mossler, and if the strike killed him. Maybe it depends on the force involved. I'm well aware that karate strikes can be quite powerful.

I took Tae Kwon Do for four years, earning a brown belt, and I once attended a lesson with the grand master of the schools. A smallish Japanese man, he demonstrated a move by punching me lightning-fast in the stomach. It felt as if I'd been whacked with an eight-pound sledgehammer that stopped after entering my belly a quarter inch. If he'd struck full force, my tummy would've felt like a dropped bowl of Jell-O.

Makes me think of the power with which an asteroid or comet can hit the Earth, wiping out terrestrial life. The scary part being that we can't predict with certainty when and where they're coming. Only that they're on their way. Not long ago, the Toutatis asteroid, an hourglass-shaped rock about one and a half miles wide and three miles long, passed within less than a million miles of Earth, which is like a whisker's width in the Universe. Had it struck our dear planet, I wouldn't be concerned about crime in America.

About 700 asteroids a kilometer or so wide are circling near the Earth, and a collision with any of them would wipe out human civilization. Perhaps a hundred million asteroids of twenty meters or larger, each capable of destroying cities the size of New York, are in line to cross our orbit. Hillsboro wouldn't stand a chance.

So I have respect for the damage that an asteroid or a karate blow can do. And I surmise that a karate strike may be more deadly than the coroner would realize. Still, the decision as to a cause of death is up to him.

Besides, David said he didn't hit Mossler. He recalled Mossler grabbed at his neck, collapsed, then struck his throat on the door frame. So maybe Mossler was already dying when he fell, and the smack on the door was coincidental.

I think I'll interview Pete Sanders, the kid who owns the house where the meeting was held. Maybe he knows more than what he said in his statement to the cops. At least he can fill me in on the reason for the argument between David and Mossler.

On the way to Sanders's house, my Trailblazer veers off Wanamaker on to a street which I notice is the one where the law offices of Amy Harrington sit in legalistic repose. Damn the coincidences of life. They make logical reality such a farce.

As long as I'm so close, I reason, I may as well contact Ms. Harrington, since she's involved in this matter, as am I, and we'll definitely have to keep tabs on what each of us is doing in the case. I park, shuffle along the short sidewalk, and enter the quiet office space. The blonde receptionist pops her gum and adjusts her strained shirt front as I approach, then gives me her standard 300-watt smile and asks what she can do for me.

"I'd like to speak with Ms. Harrington, if she's available."

I can almost hear the gears whirring behind that unlined brow. "Her one-thirty just left. She's got a hearing at three, but maybe she'll squeeze you in. Just a sec."

I wait just a sec, then a few more secs as she turns away, speaks into her headset, one glaring red fingernail tapping at the console in front of her, while with her other hand she brushes back a wisp of blonde hair. She chats, nods her head, punches a button in front of her. Looking up, she says, "Go on back. She'll see you now."

I thank her and gather my numb leg for the journey down the hall. The oak-paneled door's ajar, and I peek in, spotting what I'd been thinking about the past hour—the porcelain face and short dark hair framing a killer smile and dancing, intelligent chestnut eyes. My heart actually flutters.

"Come in, Max. My, it's been a while." She stands behind her gleaming oak desk and offers her hand, which, as that's all being offered, I eagerly clutch and shake.

"Too long," I say cleverly. She smells of hints of honey-suckle. Devastating. "How've you been, counselor?" Ever the suave cosmopolitan.

"Just fine, thanks. You know, I was just thinking that with this new snowfall it's probably beautiful out at your place."

"It's a crystal palace, like Superman's lair at the north pole."

"I'd love to see it."

30

I hesitate. Amy's a fine woman. Smart, pretty, easy to talk to. I know Sharon would want me to get to know her, she always wanted the best for me. Urged me to go on with my life, live it to the fullest, be happy.

"Yes," I say, suddenly getting cold feet, "we'll have to do that sometime."

Still, I'm imagining Amy and myself viewing the stars with my Celestron telescope. Later we could sip champagne as we recline before a foot-warming fire. I wonder if she likes sledding?

"Yes, well, have a seat. Anything new on Jeff's son?"

I tell her what I've been doing, what I've found out, and what I intend to do next.

"So we're in the initial phases," she summarizes, correctly.

"That's about it."

"I told Jeff I'd do whatever I could for his son," she says.

"I'm glad we'll be working together again."

She seems puzzled, not sure how to read that comment. She nods, then glances at her watch—attractive, slim, expensive-looking. Much like her.

She gives me a fleeting look, then says, "Sorry, I'm going to have to cut this short. I've got to get to David's hearing."

I'm pretty sure I detected a note of regret.

"Right. So, I'll talk with you later." Maybe I should ask her out now. What could it hurt? I stand up, look at her, breathe heavily. Quiet reigns.

"All right, Max, we'll be in touch. Let me know what you find out, and I'll keep you posted on the court proceedings."

Ah, hell.

Sanders's house is a three-bedroom ranch in Lake Sherwood, a nice neighborhood in southwest Hillsboro. Expensive digs for such a young man. But Jeff told me these kids are doing well with their company, and money seems to be attracted to computer-techish ideas. At least it was, before the plummet in the market. But maybe it's coming back.

I exit my SUV, noting the surroundings. The sun's out, and the snow's melted a bit, but I can make out the place where David and Mossler stood beside the Porsche. Still doesn't look as if they had a fight there.

I examine the garage, then follow the sidewalk to the front of the house. After I punch the doorbell a couple of times, Pete opens up, and I introduce myself. He's medium height, thin, with curly dark hair that frames a severe face, rather like a ferret. Silver wire-rim glasses. Handshake perfunctory and weak.

"Sorry to keep you waiting, I wasn't sure that was the doorbell," he says. "I was back in my office cracking into the Pentagon mainframe."

I must look surprised, because his mouth twists into a sly grin.

I smile. "You got me, didn't you?"

"I heard you were ex-FBI. You're an easy target."

"Hey, I'm not as uptight as some."

"That's good, come on in. What do you need?"

I study him a moment. "As you know, I'm working with the police on Kyle Mossler's death. I wanted to talk with you about what you saw."

He motions me to follow. We settle into some department store furniture—turquoise, burgundy, beige—he in a recliner and I on the sofa. I decline the offer of a drink, and Sanders watches me for a moment, waiting for my questions, a self-assured young man.

"Pete, could you tell me what the meeting was about?"

He shifts in the chair and cracks his knuckles. "It was a

business discussion. We've been branching out into a new area of security programs, and we were assessing developments."

"Something to do with the use of special encryption techniques and embedded Trojans?"

He looks startled; David must've been giving me the straight scoop. "In a way. It's rather experimental and highly technical. Plus, I'll have to mention, extremely confidential."

I nod, saying, "I see." But I'm rather in the dark. "How many people are in your company?"

"Just the six . . . I mean, five of us. We may expand, depending on future orders. But for now, we mostly work from home."

"And you've all got E-mail, I assume."

"Sure."

"Then why the face-to-face meeting?"

"We get together once a month. We're friends, as well as business partners."

"How did you guys meet?"

"Several of us were in college together. The others we met through chat rooms on the Net, followed by E-mail discussions. We all got together in Denver a couple of years ago and decided to form a company."

"Even though several of the partners are from out-of-state?"

"That doesn't matter these days—with computer connections, cell phones, faxes."

"Of course." I flip a page in my notebook. "You told the police you saw David hit Mossler."

He freezes for a tick, but readjusts quickly to my sudden shift of subject. "I said I glanced outside, saw David's arm go toward Kyle, then saw Kyle drop."

"You saw Mossler collapse?"

"Yes, I saw him go down."

"Does he do that a lot?"

He squints and pushes up his glasses. I wait for his ferret-like nose to twitch, but he stays composed. "What do you mean?"

"I was wondering why you didn't go outside to help him."

He crosses his legs. "I was going to, but David ran back here, banged on the door, and told me to call 9-1-1."

"Which you did."

"Yes, of course."

"What'd you tell them?"

"That Kyle passed out."

"Could you see that his eyes were closed?"

"Well, no. It was too far for that."

"But you could clearly see David and him standing by the car?"

"Sure."

"The porch light was on?"

"Right. And the one out by the garage."

I stand, walk to the door, then peer out the window beside it. "How far would you say it is to the driveway from here?"

He crosses to where I am, looks through the glass, then says, "I'd guess a dozen yards."

"Yeah, that's about what it looks like to me." I stepped it off as thirty-two feet to the door. "Now could you do something for me?"

His eyes show he's miffed, but he tries to look cordial and cooperative. "I can try. What do you want?"

"Open the door."

"This door?"

"Yes."

"Open it?"

"If you would."

He sighs with a hint of exasperation, then pulls it open.

"How long would you say that took you?"

"To open the door?"

"Yes."

"About two seconds. Why?"

I pinch my lower lip, then look out the window again.

"Just follow my thinking here. Mossler collapses, David checks to see if he's breathing and has a pulse. Then he runs back here, knocks, and tells you to call 9-1-1."

"That's right."

"Before you can open the door?"

He stares at me for a long second. "You know, I didn't say I looked out that window."

Damn. "Where did you look out?"

"From my office at the far end of the house. So after I'd watched a few seconds to see if Kyle was going to get up, then hustled in here, David was already at the door."

"So that accounts for the delay."

"I'd say so."

"Could you show me which window you looked out?"

He blows a breath through his nostrils and straightens his glasses. "Come on."

So much for being cordial. At least he's still cooperative. When he turns away, I flip up the two switches beside the door.

We hike down the hallway to the last room, an office with an oversized desk laden with computer equipment. It's stocked with new wooden file cabinets with shiny brass handles, a comfortable-looking swivel chair, and a couple of telephones. Two modern lamps provide a soft glow on the desktop.

There's a window beside the desk.

"This one," he says.

I lift up the mini-blind and peer out into the front yard. Then I turn my head to glimpse the driveway. At least, the back part of it. The front part, where the Porsche was parked, is blocked by a large bush.

"I can't see too well," I say.

"Why not?" he says, as though I'm batty.

"Take a look."

He sniffs, then hoists the blinds with a sharp snap of the cord. Glances at me, then looks out. "Umm." He moves over to the far edge of the window.

Then he stares at the floor, shoots a glimpse across the room, and says, "Now that I think about it, I was just coming in here to work, and I went to that fridge to get a can of pop." He's indicating a dormitory-sized refrigerator on the floor to the right of his desk. "Then I must've glanced out that other window." He makes his way there, opens the blinds and cranes his neck. "Yes, here, look, you can see the driveway fine from here."

I do. You *can* see somewhat better. But why didn't he start here?

"So, why did you look outside?"

"To make sure the guys had left. I had work to do and didn't want to be disturbed."

"I see." This is going nowhere fast. "Do you have some literature about your company?"

"I'll give you our Web address."

Swell.

As I leave, Sanders closes the door behind me, and I glance back at the porch light, which gleams in its globe. Then I amble along the sidewalk to the outside lamp at the edge of the garage, which remains dark. I lift the lid, unscrew the bulb, and shake it. Sounds like a maraca. The top's burned black. I screw it back in and replace the lid.

That explains why the crime scene photos showed the garage lamp was off when the cops arrived. It wasn't yet dark when the incident occurred, but still, with a snowstorm in progress, every bit of light makes a difference. Just as the light from a small star can breach the dark void, reaching us from billions of miles away.

Chapter 4

As I drive home, I think about the interview with Sanders. My first impression was he was lying about seeing David reach out toward, or strike, Mossler. That he heard the EMTs talking about the collapsed larynx, and, for some unknown reason, decided to try to pin the blame on David.

Only one problem: David *did* reach out to Mossler. He told me so. And if Sanders wasn't looking out the window, dead garage light or no, how would he have known to relate that scenario to the cops?

Unless it just seemed like a commonsense way to frame David, which I suppose it was, given David's proximity to Mossler and David's background in karate. Not to mention their argument. Or maybe Sanders heard David telling the cops about reaching out to Mossler, and then he concocted his story of David possibly smacking him. I'll have to resolve that enigma.

Traffic is thin, and I'm sailing along Wanamaker, watching the Sun sinking lower in the sky. Fields of snow spread in vast stretches, and trees like black candelabra grasp at the sky. There's a sense of power in the muffled fields and woods that can't be found in town among the brick and steel structures.

I love living in the country, where I'm aware of my unremarkable place in nature. One must attune to the rhythms and rules of natural life. Timber rattlesnakes, recluse spiders, and territorial hornets can punish you for your trespasses. Skunks, bobcats, and cougars are best avoided. Still, if one listens to the rumbling thunder, takes heed of the blowing snow, and admires the spring flowers, he can appreciate the symphony of life.

In town, telephones, computers, and fax machines control their human slaves. Those electronic marvels—E-mail, the Net, and cellular phones—have taken over people's lives. Perhaps so will the computer programs David mentioned.

In fact, I realize I've been sucked into an alien world where I'm sure I'll show my lack of expertise about computers and their software. I'm especially ignorant of how one plants a Trojan horse. It may not be significant regarding Mossler's death, but I've a niggling tug at the edge of my psyche that's affecting my take on this matter. It's like when the Moon, 238,000 miles distant from the Earth, affects our oceans' tides. So what to do?

I'm pretty sure Arty Carpenter and Hal Owen won't have any experience or interest in those fields, either. Of course, some of my FBI contacts may be knowledgeable. In fact, I heard that Marisol Vegas, my sweetheart from distant days in Puerto Rico, had left sunny Miami for a desk job at FBIHQ in D.C., heading the computer fraud section.

But first I want to bone up on ways to invade or take over people's computers. I've found it helps to be able to understand experts if you're not totally ignorant about the subject at hand. My earlier detour by the library netted me several books on the matter, so I'm ready to get educated.

As I pull into my long gravel driveway, I note that everything looks pretty much as I left it. Lugging the weighty material into the house, I let Binga inside where she sniffs at her dog bowl in case the dog food fairy paid a visit while she was guarding the porch. I drop the tomes on the kitchen counter, hit the fridge for a cold pop, and notice my message machine's blinking.

I pop a top and take a refreshing swig, then punch the play button. "You have two new messages," says the robot girl. Wow, a personal best.

Amy called to advise that David's arraignment resulted in his being bound over for a preliminary hearing, but that he was released from custody on bond.

I'm glad he's out. Maybe I can talk to him again in a couple of days, when I have a better handle on this situation, and he'll give me a little more helpful information. Perhaps.

Or maybe the coroner will rule Mossler's death accidental. Or a drug overdose. Or an aneurysm that burst.

Who knows?

The second message is a voice I don't recognize. I check caller ID, which shows the number that called is blocked. The message is short and enigmatic.

"Longfellow told us, 'When it's raining, it is best to let it rain.' Technology can be dangerous if you're not familiar with it, Mr. Austin. It's better if you don't delve too deeply and get burned." Click.

I stare at the machine a moment, then replay the message, listening more carefully. Sounds like a white male in his forties, East Coast accent, educated, uses good grammar, no discernible background noises. What in the world is that all about?

I hit the buttons for redialing the last number that called. But I get a recording, telling me it doesn't work for that number. Bleeped again.

Carrying the computer books into the living room, I collapse into my leather chair, and, contrary to recent advice, begin to delve into the technology of computer pirating. "Never hurts to learn something new," I mutter. Hope I'm right about that.

★ ★ ★ ★ ★

A couple of hours spent reading, with brief time-outs to fix Binga her dinner and to grab myself some spicy peanuts and a cold beer, and I've absorbed all I can concerning computer takeovers.

There are various procedures used, most of them working through the Internet. Spyware, malware, adware, spybots, cookies, viruses, worms—all can be introduced into or "infect" one's computer and perform a myriad of unsavory functions.

A user can pick up these bugs by opening E-mail attachments, or by downloading free games, music, or other intriguing files such as supposed photos of sexy girls. They are even attached to files that are otherwise helpful to the user, such as ones that upgrade one's ability to view graphics or videos. Once a computer is infected, the "cracker" in charge of the bug will have complete access to the system.

He'll be able to execute commands on the infected computer, as well as access, download, or delete any files. The infiltrator can intercept passwords, get into records that reveal one's personal background information such as Social Security number, bank account numbers, and credit card numbers. And they can literally "hijack" a person's computer, using it to send E-mails or files to other unsuspecting users, thereby infecting their computers, as well.

"This sucks!" I say.

Binga lifts her head from her doggy mat, looking at me with distress in her large brown orbs, which seems to signal I'm acting daffier than usual.

"I'm just appalled at the minuscule limits of man's decency and integrity," I explain.

She lets out a long sigh, then returns to her meditative pose.

I flip a page and return to my research. Here's a great one: intruders can install a dialer as the browser address for your Internet service provider, often calling sites (usually porn ones) that bill you a hefty fee for accessing them. Some of these evil devices are even incorporated in some common software programs. The bugs monitor your interests, your choices in sites you call up, and what you shop for. All intended to sell to companies who want to target you with ads about items you seem predisposed to buy.

So much invasion. And David mentioned the use of a Trojan horse in their computer security software program. Which has been sold to companies and government bodies. Many secrets can be compromised. An icy sensation floods my body, almost stopping my heart. Maybe the security and well-being of America is at risk.

The morning air is clear and cold, with a crispness that brings my senses alert. I'm standing on the side porch, my breath vaporizing before me, while Binga hobbles across the gravel driveway, squats and poops. Thank goodness I live in the country and don't have to follow her with a scooper. If it becomes necessary, there's a shovel in the garage. Otherwise, hey, fahgeddaboudit.

Anyway, I don't traipse around barefoot in summer. At least not in spots where the grass hasn't been mowed in a while. I learned that the hard way.

Nevertheless, I've found life in the country to be stimulating and satisfying. Closeness to nature is something mankind has let fade from ordinary experience. Many people are too busy surfing the Net, watching TV, or talking on cell phones to watch finches and redbirds flit from treetop to treetop.

Which makes it all the more a pity that I've been drawn

into this case, with its obvious ramifications of complex computer technology, possibly involving cracking or virus infusion. But I wouldn't be in this position if it weren't for David's involvement. And perhaps the tech weenie aspect of this matter has nothing to do with Mossler's death.

Still, I'm almost positive there's some connection with the corporate group, Zipdata. One of their members dead, two interviewed about the killing, both of whom are possibly lying or covering up. Leaves me with three more partners to contact.

A breeze lifts my hair, giving me a slight chill. The Sun has emerged above the horizon as a huge red ball, ready to begin its low arc across the southern sky. Binga comes back, panting, ready for her dog biscuit reward for a job well done.

I'll fix myself a couple of fried eggs, shower and dress, then head downtown to talk with the detectives to see if they have anything new. Then I'll stop for a chat with the coroner.

After that I'll make some calls. The remaining young men in the company live in San Francisco, Denver, and San Antonio. I'll have to plan how to interview them.

I glance at the phone, recalling my mysterious message. Without the recorder on my phone, the jerk wouldn't have been able to threaten me. He'd have had to talk to me directly, if he'd had the—

"For heaven's sake," I exclaim. Telephone recorders. Of course. The dispatcher at the police station will have a recording of Sanders's 9-1-1 call. I can listen to that to see if he said anything about David hitting Mossler.

And, now that I think about it, Kyle Mossler's funeral is tomorrow. The other kids in the corporation will likely be there, as will I. Not that I'm so gauche as to conduct business on the same day as the funeral, but perhaps I can at least set up some appointments.

I pull the electric skillet out of the bottom cabinet, accidentally dislodging a couple of pot lids which clang loudly on the tile floor. "Damn," I comment. Ears ringing, I grab a couple, oh, heck, make it three, eggs from the fridge. Butter, milk, and a few frozen sausages. Turn on the skillet, pour in a little safflower oil, and pop some wheat bread into the toaster.

And the kitchen lights and appliances all go dead. "Good grief," I say, recalling that I can't run the toaster and the skillet at the same time. So I unplug the toaster, then walk into the mudroom and flip the appropriate switch on the circuit breaker board.

Makes me wonder what might happen if too many people accessed the Net at the same time. Could that all go kaplooey, too? Can a billion Web sites vanish into thin air?

Like my ancient electrical system, I wonder if we're all becoming too interconnected. I know I wouldn't flourish in these days of twenty-four-hour contact with one's company, business acquaintances, customers, friends, and bill collectors. A person needs time alone for reflection, rumination, and relaxation. Quiet time. Time to meditate. To think. To veg out or, as they say now, to chill.

I glance at Binga, who's staring at me, waiting for some meaningful communication. Or, perhaps, for me to drop some food on the floor. "Once this case is over," I assure her, "we'll take a nice vacation."

She looks doubtful. Even fretful. Does she sense something I don't?

Anyway, sometime today I'll check out the Web site for Zipdata, Inc. Then I'll call Marisol tonight with whatever questions I've developed, and for any suggestions or insights she may have in this situation. When in techie land, use a good techie guide, I always say—especially if she happens to be gorgeous.

Chapter 5

Before I leave the house, I need to get my case reports in order. Plopping down at my PC, I type in the results of the interviews I did with David and Pete Sanders, as well as my take on the crime scene, then print out three copies. I punch holes in one and put it in a binder where I've inserted copies of the officers' reports and crime scene photos. The others are for the detectives working the case.

Then I grab my sports coat, toss the binder into a canvas carry case, and leave the house, with Binga scooting outside ahead of me. I thought she was slowing down, but maybe not yet. Good for her.

As I cruise along Burlingame Road in my SUV, lost in a fogbank of daydreaming, a deer leaps from some woods and darts across the road ahead. Slamming on the brakes, I skid on the snow covering the asphalt. But my rumbling ride stops in time, and with my heart thumping like a rabbit's, I watch the doe bound away, its white tail waving good-bye.

Accelerating, I watch the road more closely now, while pondering how close I came to striking that poor deer dead in its tracks, as drivers do many times each year. It would've been a bolt from the blue, as far as the deer was concerned. And as I consider sudden death on this Earthly sphere, I see the similarity to what happened to Mossler.

I'm wondering if it was simply an accidental death. Or if he died by natural causes. Hey, maybe the kid got zapped with a laser beam from an alien spacecraft.

I have a warped mind, sometimes. And I suppose occasionally it serves me well. Although, in the FBI, it tended to get me in trouble more often than not; no original thinking was favored or rewarded by the bureaucratic system.

But since I'm left pretty much to my own devices now, I try to come up with creative reasoning whenever possible. Sometimes it works. And sometimes it gets me stuck in a vortex of whirling possibilities that might suck me into oblivion, like a black hole swallowing entire star systems.

But without further mishap, I roll into the police station lot, breathe a sigh of relief, and bound from my ride like a young buck, twisting my knee in the process. Jeez. I slam the door and limp toward the glass doors, trying to ignore the sharp pain in my meniscus.

Arty Carpenter comes to the front to escort me to the squad room. When we enter, I see Paula Jackson seated at her desk, and in passing I notice her calves, which have an artful, muscular curvature. She looks up, and I give her a smile.

She smiles back and nods, then tugs at her skirt as she crosses her legs. Caught again. I hope she realizes I'm only admiring the beauty she's adding to the world.

"Hey, Max, what's shaking?" asks Owen, who strolls over and drops into a chair beside Arty's desk. He's looking exceptionally dapper, with a blue pinstripe suit and a sharp red-on-blue tie. And he's sure more cheerful than his usual acerbic mood.

"Nothing with me. Now, the Earth had that wobble about eighty-four million years ago."

"Huh?"

"Yeah, the planet shook, and it reversed the magnetic polarity for a couple million years. But since then, all's been steady."

He adjusts his tie, a frown on his face. "I meant how you been doin'."

"Oh, of course. Fine, Hal. And you?"

"Better and better, the broads tell me." His sanguine grin reappears.

"That settles that Earth-shaking controversy."

His brow creases. "Yeah, I suppose."

Arty drops into his chair, watching us banter, a serious look on his face, which strikes me as unusual. He's typically quite placid. A stone in the river around which water flows without much effect.

"Anything 'shaking' on the Mossler murder?" I ask Arty.

"Still waiting for the coroner's report. I checked this morning, and he says he'll have it finished soon."

"I'll go by and give him some grief. Maybe he'll give it up."

"Yeah," agrees Owen, "he always has to cross them *t*'s and everything in his reports. As if anyone cares." He chuckles to himself. "I know the stiffs don't give a big rat's ass."

"Maybe the next-of-kin want it done right," I say, though I realize Owen is just blowing smoke. Somehow, he gets under my never-thick-enough skin. The jerk.

"So what you got for us?" Owen says, pointedly. "Or is this the usual one-way street, like when you worked for the feds?"

"Not at all, 'partner.' We're all in this cozy crime-busting cartel together." I hand Arty a manila envelope. "My interviews and observations thus far," I say. "Anything else I get I'll hand right over." Although I don't think I'll mention the threatening phone call at the moment.

Owen nods, impressed, I think, but not willing to admit it. "Hey, we got something for you, too." He looks at Arty, who has pulled my reports from the envelope and is handing pages to Owen.

"Oh, yeah," Arty says, opens a desk drawer, and extends a handsome multicolored binder, much higher quality than the red one in my carry case.

I examine it, finding it contains the officers' reports, as well as revised reports from both detectives, more crime scene photos than they originally provided, statements taken with the EMTs, and a statement from the examiner who pronounced David dead at the scene.

"Very nice," I say. "Thanks."

Arty says, "You're wel—"

"You contacted the out-of-state kids yet?" Owen interrupts.

"Not yet. Maybe tomorrow."

"At the funeral?"

"That's what I was thinking. But just to set up something."

"Us, too. The uniforms got statements from them the day of the murder, saying they hadn't seen anything. But we want to interview them ourselves."

"They've already left town?"

"Yeah, they took off the morning after the killing. We tried to call them, but all we got so far is answering machines."

"Did you e-mail them?"

Owen stares at me quizzically.

"No," says Arty, then clears his throat. "We'll get hold of them, though. Do you want to sit in on our interviews?"

Not really. I always like to ask my own questions. But I'm in an awkward situation here.

"That'd be fine," I say. Then I slip the new binder into my carry case, zip it, and watch as Arty inserts the pages I gave him into a cheap black binder on his desk.

"How come I get this fancy one?" I say.

Arty blinks and looks at Owen.

"The chief said you should have it," Owen says.

I glance at Arty, who's nodding.

"Nice of him," I say.

"For some reason he wants to stay on your good side," Owen explains in a strained attempt at a diplomatic manner.

I didn't know I had a bad side. Aw, hell. Yes, I did.

"Been a pleasure working with you gents. I'm going to check with the coroner, as I said, then I'll be contacting some computer experts."

"What for?" asks Owen, fidgeting in his chair.

"So I can understand more about what the Zipdata company was doing."

They exchange a glance, as though they're thinking: *What's this goober up to?*

"Do you think," Arty says hesitantly, "that has anything to do with what happened to the Mossler kid?"

"I think there's a possibility."

"Anything's possible," says Owen—Mr. Agreeable—with a small snort. "But what we got here seems pretty open and shut, once we get confirmation from the coroner on cause of death. Then we can close down this little tragedy, just like in *Hamlet*, or some of those Shakespeare things you read."

Gee, a literary reference from Owen. Will wonders never cease? And then I get a flash of my own. "Maybe more appropriate is the Shakespearian quote: 'Woe to the hand that shed this costly blood.' At least, that's my goal here."

They look at me strangely, so I get up, say my good-byes, and take my leave.

As I'm making my retreat, Detective Jackson stands up from her desk, smooths her skirt, then picks up a matching jacket and a black binder.

"You leaving?" I ask cleverly.

She regards me with those clarion blue eyes. "Yes, I am. Can I walk you out?"

"I'm not going far, but I'd enjoy your company."

She gives me a quick smile. Then she assumes the look of a tough female detective heading out to kick criminal butt. What can this mean?

In the hallway, I ask her, "How long have you been a detective?" She wasn't here a couple of years ago.

"About a year and a half," she says. "In Hillsboro, that is. I worked for the Miami PD for seven years. I'd been a detective there for two. Then I transferred here, and they decided they could use my expertise."

"And what's that?" I ask.

But she's looking down the hall at a man and a woman approaching us, and I glance in that direction. Chief Brighton, a tall, beefy man who wears the uniform and his years on the force with a calm assurance, pushes back the gray hair at one temple as he bends down to catch something his much-shorter secretary is telling him.

"Hello, Chief," Paula says brightly, then nods to Arliss.

I greet them, too.

"Ah, Paula . . . and Austin." The chief smiles, not at me. He's no dummy.

Arliss, a plain woman with plenty of laps around the track, doesn't seem too thrilled to see the good detective. But she greets both of us politely.

Now the chief hesitantly shifts his gaze to me. "Thanks for lending us a hand on the Mossler case," he says. "That's a touchy matter for us, of course. I'm glad we've got your experience and contacts."

"No problem, Chief. Anything to help Jeff's kid."

He nods gravely.

"And thanks for the binder," I say. "It'll keep me up

on what your guys are doing."

I see a question mark appear above his head, but after a quick peek at Arliss, who doesn't shrug, but may as well have, he says, "Sure thing, Austin. Whatever you need, just ask Arliss, and she'll fix you up."

"That's great, Chief."

As they amble down the hall, I say, "The chief seems to like you, Paula."

"He's a man, isn't he?" A smile plays at the corners of her mouth.

You got me there. By the way, what was your criminal specialty?"

She rolls her eyes and sighs. "Vice and sexual assaults. In Miami they had me play a prostitute, plus listen to the horror stories of female rape vics."

"Ah . . . sure, I can see you as a compassionate interviewer."

She slows by the exit door. "Max, that was the right thing to say. No 'hooker' jokes. Thanks for the respect."

"I don't know any reason you don't deserve it."

"Most guys around here don't understand that female prerequisite. They think strutting their buff stuff will conquer all the adoring bimbos."

I shrug. "Different strokes," I say. "I haven't got much to strut."

She eyes me up and down. "Don't sell yourself short."

"I'll take that as a compliment. Now, you be careful out there."

"I will," she says with a smile that brightens the corridor. "And if you have any problems on this case, I'll be glad to help."

"Deal," I say, and watch her depart. She's hinting that something may be slippery in this case, but I've no idea what. Which intrigues me. And rouses me to plunge headlong into the fray, seeking the pure, blazing truth.

51

Chapter 6

Still wondering what Paula meant by her cryptic comment about "problems" on the case, I ease into the dispatcher's office. Fortunately, I know the woman working here today, and she finds the reel where Pete Sanders made the 9-1-1 call about Kyle Mossler collapsing. I listen to it. He only talks about Mossler fainting. Nothing about David striking him.

Not sure whether that means anything or not, I thank her and proceed down the hall. Now I'm approaching the coroner's door. Hiking up the canvas bag on my shoulder, I think about questions to ask.

Gunther Wahrmach is the forensic pathologist who's involved in this seemingly strange death, but he's not in his office. So I head toward the autopsy rooms. Suddenly he exits one, walking toward me with his gaunt bald pate leading the way. He seems lost in thought, studying the floor as he stalks along on thin, spidery legs. Then he senses me in the hallway and looks up, his mouth partly open, startled.

After all the horrors he's seen, I marvel that anything alarms him.

"Ah, Max, I didn't see you there." He compresses his lips, then continues, "Although I heard you were working on the Mossler case, and I've been expecting you to show up."

"I believe I've been a model of patience not bugging you before now. Such restraint should deserve a reward."

He rubs the back of his head, then adjusts his pewter-colored wire-rim glasses and says, "Fine. Come to my office. I've got some results for you."

"Anything peculiar?" I ask, not really sure why.

"You put your finger upon that one."

With Gunther, you have to interpret his syntax liberally, but it's often that way with intellectuals.

Settling behind his desk, which has papers and journals and reports stacked in profusion, he leans back in his chair. With his hands clasped before him, his index fingers extended, he touches his lips, a study in contemplation. Maybe he's a closet Buddhist.

"Did you finish the workup?" I ask.

He nods firmly. "I'm just about done with it. It's a fascinating case."

Now I'm on alert. For Gunther to be so expressive, it might mean something that'll shock me out of my briefs. "What've you got?"

"Did you notice the blue skin tint in the crime scene photos?"

"Now that you mention it."

He makes a guttural noise, then goes on. "The boy died of sudden respiratory failure."

"So he *did* have a damaged larynx?" I'm getting a sick feeling.

"He did."

"Caused by a blow?"

"Of course, of some sort, I would think."

"But you don't know if it was a karate blow, or from striking the car door?"

He lifts his shoulders slightly, then drops them. "Hard to tell such a thing. There wouldn't be much difference."

"But if that's what killed Mossler—"

He holds up a hand. Almost a Nazi salute. But surely he wasn't—

"I didn't say that was the reason he died."

My jaw drops an inch. I squint at him, trying to comprehend. "Wait a minute. You said he couldn't get enough air, and his larynx was impaired."

"True enough. As far as it goes."

"Then what else?"

He shuffles some papers on his desk, and I'm pretty sure it's a transcript of his examination of Mossler. With a bony index finger, he pushes his glasses higher on his hawk-like beak. He reads a few lines, then dips his head and peers at me over the tops of his glasses with icy green eyes.

I feel a definite chill.

"His liver was inflamed. Not typical for a healthy young man."

"Liquor? Drugs?"

He tilts his head from side to side, his thin lips pursed. "In a manner of speaking. It was *Strychnos toxifera*."

"Jesus, Gunther. What the hell is that?"

"Curare."

Now he watches me. A skinny, featherless hawk with cheaters. I feel like a mouse caught in an open field, going into shock.

"Did you say . . . curare?" I've read about flying death. Used on darts by South American natives to paralyze or kill animals or tribal enemies.

"I told you it was fascinating. Even bizarre."

"It's more than that. It's . . . *unbelievable*. How sure are you?"

"The spectrograph gave that reading. Pure science, Max."

I'm shaking my head, my mind spinning like a centrifuge. "Mossler was poisoned?"

"Yah, absolutely."

"Someone put it in his drink?"

He waggles a thin hand in dismissal. "No, no, nothing like that. One can drink curare, and it won't kill them."

"Then how?"

"It has to be injected."

Swell.

"Gunther, I don't recall a syringe being found at the scene."

He's nodding again. "Good observation. You're on the track, now."

"So what happened?"

He comes as close to smiling as I've ever seen him. "There was a slight perforation in his neck. Actually, the puncture hit his carotid artery."

Are we talking vampires now?

Gunther is in his element, talking as though reciting a journal article. "With such direct introduction into the bloodstream, the death certainly occurred right away. Though curare kills almost immediately, anyway."

"How did he die?" I croak out, stunned.

"Paralysis of the diaphragm, the pulse rate plummets, then there's paralysis of the lungs. The victim can't breathe. It's like he's drowning on dry land."

What a way to go. Of course, death has a heartless way of never being a walk in the park. At least, that's my indirect observation.

"So how did someone spike Mossler in the neck with curare, then get rid of the murder weapon?"

"You're the investigator. I was hoping you'd figure out that part."

I blow out a breath. "I always get the easy grounders."

Gunther promises he'll complete his written report by tomorrow. As I leave his office, stunned, I'm scrambling to come up with a hypothesis on this strange murder. This may be that black hole I was dreading.

Then I spot Arty. He also has a stricken look on his face. What's up? I wonder.

"Oh, Max. I'm glad I caught you."

"Hey, I just talked to Gunther."

"What'd he say?"

"He said Mossler died from poisoning by curare."

He stares at me and jangles the change in his pocket. Then his expression lightens. "I sorta suspected voodoo myself. *Really,* what'd he say? I'm very curious."

I jerk my head, and we move to the side of the hallway as some people walk past. "I'm serious, man. Gunther said a lab test confirmed it."

Now he looks thoroughly puzzled. "Like that poison that pygmies in Africa use?"

"Close enough."

"Someone spiked his drink?"

"No, someone spiked him. It has to be injected."

"What?"

"Has to go into the bloodstream."

"You're shittin' me."

"Arty, listen, this is for real."

"But there was no needle at the scene. Do you think someone shot him up in the house? Or he thought he was doing H, and he somehow got some bad shit?"

"No, he got hit in the carotid. Death happened real quick. It had to have happened outside."

"But how? David had nothing on him, and we didn't spot anything in the vicinity. You think he tossed it?"

"I don't know. We can check it out."

"I'll get Owen."

★ ★ ★ ★ ★

Within a half hour, we're back at Sanders's house. No car there, no answer to our ringing of his bell. So we search around the yard, street, and driveway. We even plunge into bushes and thrash through some mulch in the flower beds. Nothing.

"I suppose he could've lobbed it onto the roof," Owen says.

"Yeah," Arty says, his hands on his hips, neck craning upward, "but how would we get up—"

And Sanders pulls into the driveway in his Toyota 4Runner. He climbs out, peering at first the detectives, then me. "What's going on?" he says.

"We need to check the crime scene again," I say. "Make sure we didn't miss anything."

"Okay," he says. "You need anything?"

He's more helpful today. "Got a ladder? We need to take a look on the roof."

His brow furrows, but he simply says, "Sure. In the garage." He reaches into his Toyota, points a black door opener, and up she goes.

I set up the ladder at a strategic point, then we trained investigators all stare at each other for several long seconds.

"Oh, hell," says Owen, "I'll go up." And he does, rather athletically, I think. Though he seems more tentative once he plants his feet on the roof's incline.

"I've got some work to do, if you don't need anything else," Sanders tells us.

"Fine with me," I say.

Arty says, "Sure. Go ahead."

As we watch him disappear into the house, Arty says, "I've got something new. We'll have to tell Sanders about it before we leave."

"Hit me."

"We got through on one of the other kids' phones. Wade Lawrence, lives in Denver?"

I nod. "Did you set up an interview?"

"I didn't talk with him. There was a homicide dick at his house."

My mouth feels like I've swallowed a handful of dust. "You mean—"

"He went jogging in a park near his house. Had a cardiac arrest."

Now I'm getting that spinning feeling again. "That's death by natural causes. Why the detective?"

"The patrolman who answered the squeal almost wrote it off. But a wit said she saw a man approach the Lawrence boy before he dropped."

"What?"

"She was coming around a corner, saw this guy run out of the bushes and get in the kid's way."

"Like he'd been laying for him?"

"Right. So he holds something up to the kid's face, Lawrence drops, and the guy takes off."

"Damn."

"The wit checked on the young man and found he was dead. She started screaming, and someone came along with a cell phone."

"And the man?"

"Ran back into the bushes. No trace."

"Hey, you guys," Owen yells, and we look up. He's brushing off his hands. "I been all over topside, checked the gutters, and I ain't seen shit. There's not a damn thing up here."

Isn't that the way some days? However, after puzzling this situation out, I have to say I didn't expect we'd find a syringe or dart or whatever around here. Young men, at least those without medical training, simply wouldn't kill one another in such a bizarre manner.

Not that the improbable doesn't often happen, just to show us we know nothing.

Chapter 7

I watch the detectives leave. They said they'll try to reach the other two kids in the Zipdata company and also give David and Jeff Bagley a heads-up about the second killing, just in case there's some odd intrigue going on. I'm one of the few investigators I know who believes coincidences *do* happen, but still, in this matter, I'm suspicious.

Pete Sanders gives me no further help.

"Sorry, I don't remember any strangers hanging around the neighborhood," he says. "Guess I don't watch for that sort of thing."

He adds that he doesn't worry about burglars in the area. Seldom looks out his window. Sure, except when it comes to pointing the finger at David.

Back in my SUV I ponder the situation, leafing through the colorful binder the detectives gave me. Two healthy kids die within two days, in separate cities, attacked by someone in strange ways. They belong to the same company which provides security programs to government agencies and private corporations, and the programs may have been compromised.

Could the nexus for this mini–crime wave be the Zipdata company? Or is there even a connection? Perhaps I'm just hatching a wild conspiracy theory with no real basis.

I'm more of a believer in Occam's razor, where the simplest explanation for how something may have happened is usually the right one. Which automatically rules out conspiracy theories. But there's a tingling at the back of my head signaling something bizarre could be afoot.

I grab up my cell phone and punch in Jeff Bagley's number.

"Max! The guys told me about the kid in Denver. You think David's in danger?"

"I don't know, Jeff. I don't have a handle on this yet."

"Maybe I'll have him stay at my place a few days."

"Probably a good idea. Although, I suppose if they were after him, they'd have hit him at the same time as Kyle Mossler."

"They?"

"You know I have a wild imagination. Plus, I'm thinking there was a getaway driver. Sort of a quick hit and go."

"Good point. Anyway, the chief said I could work the case now. They're dropping the charges on David, unless something else comes up."

"Do you want me to stay on it?"

"Has a cat got an ass?"

Last time I checked. "Then get out here to Sanders's house."

Once Jeff arrives, we start canvassing neighbors along the street. At the first house I try, next door to Sanders's place, a slim blonde wearing tight leotards and a sheen of sweat breathlessly answers the door.

"Sorry to interrupt your workout," I say, flashing my ID.

We sit in her living room, with her toweling off, her short ponytail swinging like a pendulum. The workouts seem to be sculpting her figure, though she has the advantage of youth. She can still eat chili dogs, French fries, and nachos without paying the spare tire tariff like us mature adults.

"I heard about Kyle getting killed," she says, shaking her head. "That really creeps me out."

"You knew him?"

"He was a couple years ahead of me at Hillsboro High, so I knew who he was. We didn't run in the same bunch, though."

"Know anyone who had a grudge against him?"

"You mean that might kill him?"

"Right."

"Oh, no."

"Did you see anyone different around this area prior to the murder?"

"No one I hadn't seen before. People that live here or visit."

"No strange cars?"

"Can't think of any."

"And you told the police earlier that you were gone at the time of Kyle's murder?"

"That's right. I went to hear a harpist at Barnes & Noble."

I close the binder on my lap. "All right, thanks for your—"

"But, you know, there *was* a delivery van out there a couple of times."

"When was that?"

"The afternoon Kyle got killed, and a couple of days before that."

"What kind of van?"

"Just a plain white van. I think it was a Chevy. There was something about delivery written on the side."

"FedEx or Indian Delivery?"

Her ponytail swishes side-to-side. "The name started with an 'S.' I noticed because my name's Sheri. It was all in script, and I liked the fancy lettering. Then there was an 'A,' and some other letters, but I don't recall what they were."

"See anyone in it?"

"Two men were sitting in front."

"Can you describe them?"

"I didn't look at them that close. I peeked outside and saw the van, then I waited a few seconds to see if they were coming here."

"Where were they—"

"I think they were wearing, like, these dark blue coveralls."

I make a note. "They were parked?"

"Yes, in front of Jordan's house. At least, the first time."

"Jordan?"

"Yeah, I don't know his last name. He plays guitar in some group. I heard him play at a party once, and he's pretty hot."

"Which house?"

"The blue one two doors down from the one directly across from me."

"Did they make a delivery to him?"

"Not while I watched. They were looking over here at Pete's place and my house. That's why I thought they might be coming here."

"You remember anything else about the van?"

"Just that the business name was in red letters."

"See a license tag?"

"I didn't notice it."

"How long was the van there?"

"I'm not sure. I left to go to Dillon's grocery about an hour later, and it was gone."

"And you saw the same van the afternoon of Kyle's murder?"

She wipes the crooks of her arms with the towel. "Yeah, around four in the afternoon. I just got back from jogging. They, like, drove by real slow that time. But I don't think they stopped."

"Were they looking at Pete's house again?"

"Maybe. I thought they might be checking out my butt, so I went inside real quick. You never know, these days."

"You never do."

As I leave, I see Jeff shouting to a frail elderly man who's cupping a hand to his ear. "All right, sir. Thanks for your help." He turns, spots me, and comes over.

"Get anything?" I ask.

"Nothing so far, how about you?"

"Young girl saw a delivery van twice, including the afternoon of the murder."

"Didn't see the tag or get the name of the company, and she can't describe the driver?"

"You've done this before," I say, then tell him what we've got to work with.

I try some more houses, finding two people not home and three others who saw nothing. Jeff finishes his side of the street and ambles back to my SUV. "Anything from Jordan?" I ask.

"Nah, he's a swacked-out kid with a loud guitar. Didn't see a van and had no deliveries made this week."

Much like astronomers' sightings of other planets. The van could signal great discoveries in store for us, or it might not amount to a pile of poop. Still, we have to sift through the dross to determine which.

Detective Bagley drives off, and I decide I'd better talk to Kyle Mossler's father, though it will be awkward to contact him right before the funeral. Firing up my ride, I put it on autopilot for the Clarion Way subdivision. I'm thinking he probably won't give up the information I want.

But often the difference between getting the answers you need and getting zero is in the way you ask the question.

Except this is a very touchy matter. So a lot of his response will probably depend on dumb luck.

Up the hill, winding, approaching the dizzying heights of the affluent digs where the well-to-do gather to flaunt their megabucks in a self-congratulatory manner. There are groomed yards, sprawling or multistory homes, all majestic and stately in their bearing. The things we do to prove ourselves worthy.

And how does my humble farmhouse in the country speak of me? From my perspective, very well, thanks. I think it shows I value independence and introspection, not to mention having a close relationship with nature. Besides, there's a lot less light pollution to hamper my viewing of the heavens. Seems perfect to me. Binga likes it, too.

I park at the curb, staring at the Mossler mansion. Here goes a whole bunch of nothing. But maybe Mr. Mossler will see the gravity of this problem and be willing to help.

Struggling up the steep driveway, past a gleaming new Mercedes, I admire the junipers and evergreens which, even in winter, have a lush green look. Other bushes flaunt radiant splashes of bright orange berries, while the branches of dogwoods glow hot crimson. No drabness allowed around these parts.

Now I pause at the summit of all that concrete, trying to catch my breath, then pace along a walkway leading to the carved dark wood door. With some anxiety, I ring the bell. Beethoven riff, I'd say.

And, just like that, Mr. Mossler opens the door. He exudes "successful businessman." Alert demeanor, glossy shoes, sporting a gold Rolex Oyster watch.

"Yes?"

He appears to think I'm delivering something, or asking for donations.

"Mr. Mossler, my name's Max Austin. I'm working with the police in the investigation of your son's death. I'm very sorry for your loss."

There's an uneasy space of silence.

"I've heard you're a friend of Jeff Bagley's," he says. "Are you just trying to get David off?"

"No, I want to find out who killed your son."

"You do realize his funeral is tomorrow?"

"Yes, if it weren't urgent, I wouldn't bother you now."

He takes a deep breath. Stalemate of stares, mine meant to show sincerity, his unreadable. Then his shoulders slump. "Come in, I don't have long. I'm still making arrangements for the funeral. Kyle's mother is too devastated to do anything."

We enter the living room, our footsteps silenced by the deep suppleness of luxury. I say, "I know the sudden death of your son must be agonizing."

Measuring me, he says, "It's the worst tragedy of my life. Like losing a part of my soul."

I sink into the proffered sofa as he takes a seat in a matching easy chair, the upholstery all swirls of lime and mauve, the table lamps low-lustre brass, tall, and striking. A huge white limestone fireplace commands the far wall. But even in this mesmerizing ambience of wealth, only one value matters: the cold steel of truth.

"Mr. Mossler, I worked for the FBI for twenty-five years. We were interested in finding facts. If our investigation showed a suspect wasn't involved, we were as happy to divulge his innocence as we would be to convict someone. I follow the same pattern in my P.I. work."

He fiddles with the arms of the easy chair, considering.

"For the moment, Mr. Austin, I'll give you the benefit of the doubt."

"Have you talked with the police today?"

"No, I just got back from the funeral home. There was a message from Detective Carpenter on the machine, but I haven't called him yet."

"There's been a strange development in this case."

His brow wrinkles. "What sort of development?"

"Wade Lawrence, another member of the Zipdata company, was murdered this morning in Denver."

He leans forward, seizing the chair arms. "What? I don't . . . are you telling me—"

"I'm afraid so."

"I don't get what you're saying. How . . . I mean . . ." His hand goes to his mouth, then toward me, seeking understanding. "Do you think they're connected?"

I shift on the sofa. "It's a stretch to say that now. I don't know how the Lawrence boy died."

He squints. "But you *do* know about my son? Is that why the detective called?"

This guy would've made a good cop. "Yes, we learned late this morning that Kyle was poisoned with curare."

"Curare? Poisoned? I . . . I . . . thought David hit him."

"That's doubtful. Anyway, it was curare that killed him, not a blow."

He slumps in his chair. "I don't understand. Could David have given him that?"

"We don't know how it happened. Kyle was stuck in the neck with some type of needle. The curare was injected."

"But the police said nothing about such a thing."

"We didn't know until the coroner finished the autopsy."

"And you don't think David was involved?"

"No, I don't. No syringe was found at the scene. And David had no motive."

He's staring at the floor, his skin a shade paler, wrinkles

now more pronounced, as though he's suddenly aged before my eyes.

Then he says quietly, "What do you want from me?"

"I'd like to access Kyle's computer."

"What on earth for?"

"I think something was going on in their business that may have ignited this."

Now his gaze turns stony. "I don't think I like the implication of that."

"I don't mean to be accusatory. It's just that from the information I've gathered so far, there seems to be a possible connection between—"

"Mr. Austin," he says, raising bolt upright, "I do thank you for the information about Kyle, but I can't let you try to dig up dirt to stain his memory. The poor boy's not even in the ground."

"Sir, I don't intend to disgrace anyone. Everything would be confidential, of course, but I'd like to see if—"

"Confidential matters have a way of leaking when the cops are involved. And if there was ever a trial, it would be paraded in the press. My family has a good reputation in the community, and I don't want it ruined."

"But there may be other lives at stake."

"That sounds highly speculative to me. I'm sorry, but this interview is over. Would you please leave?"

"But I—"

"Please, sir." He takes my arm and leads me toward the door.

But before departing, I say, "Just keep in mind that one of the other boys could've been killed first. If Kyle were now in danger, you'd want to know about it."

He hesitates a moment, then drops his hand.

"I'm sorry, Mr. Austin. I just can't assimilate all this right now. I have a son to bury—my only boy. I don't know if you can understand how terrible that is."

I nod. I can understand. "Please take my card, in case you want to talk more later."

He takes it, glances at it, then stuffs it in his pants pocket. "I still can't believe this happened."

The door closes behind me. I have to agree.

I drive a mile or so, leaving the upscale neighborhood, then turn into the parking lot for the closed-down Bauersfeld's grocery. I park on the expanse of asphalt at a distance from the silent buildings and kill the engine. Then I fish out the name and phone number that Arty gave me for the detective in Denver.

After I punch in the numbers, amazingly Detective Fournier answers.

I identify myself and tell him my connection to his murder case.

"That's a real jambalaya mess you cooking up there, son."

Cajun accent. Wonder what led him to the snowy slopes of Colorado?

"It does get intricate. But maybe there's no link at all. My first question would be how Lawrence died."

"That's sorta our trouble, too. The coroner's supposed to take a looksee tomorrow. Then maybe we'll get an idea. Right now, it look like his heart stopped and he croaked, like a frog hit by lightning."

"What about the man that ran up to him?"

"That's all we know. The young lady can't, or won't, tell us no more."

"Would you mind if I came there to sniff around a bit? I'll be glad to share anything I find."

"You say you used to be with the FBI?"

"Right. Over twenty years."

He heaves a long sigh. "Well, I s'pose I won't hold that against you since you out now. What the hey, a fresh pair of eyes and legs can't hurt, I don't figger. I'll try to clear it with the chief."

I give him my number. "Unless I hear otherwise from you, I'll be there by tomorrow evening. There's a funeral here in the morning."

"Hmmm. That *is* going around."

Way too much for my comfort.

Chapter 8

As I sit in a church pew, with solemn organ music floating over me, I'm contemplating the unpleasant, but undeniable, idea that death is an integral part of life. The violent demise of stars produces the planetary nebulae from which Earth and other planets develop. There'd be no living organisms on Earth without stars' fiery explosions, producing complex organic molecules of which every living thing is composed.

The soft sounds of sobbing family and friends press from all sides, giving me an empathetic ache in my heart for this loss to humanity. Dying sucks. Especially when we lose the innocents among us. And while Kyle Mossler may not have been as pure of heart and mind as a baby or infant, he was a promising young man and his parents' only son. His death deals them one of life's hardest blows.

Jeff Bagley slips in and sits beside me, his bulk like a solid and imposing boulder. He cuts me a glance. Leans over to tell me something.

But now the minister approaches the pulpit. He's tall and thin and seems psychologically centered within the vortex of whirling emotions of grief, anger, and despair. He glances at the organist, who winds down the poignant number, then he peers out over the group before him, his groomed silvery hair and rimless glasses lending authority to his calm, caring presence.

"We are here today to remember Kyle Mossler, a young

man who was taken from his family and friends so suddenly, so early in his life, and to thank God for his . . ."

I listen to the words, but my gaze is drawn to the family members at the front of the church. Their heads droop, and their shoulders occasionally shiver as the minister relates the passage of the brief life, now ended, at least on this mortal plane. His remains are before us, flesh and bones lying inside a gleaming bronze casket embossed with prayerful hands.

I feel a growing anger; injustice has always riled me. Sociologists and psychiatrists theorize that firstborn and only children are often shackled with an earnestness concerning life's canons of right and wrong. They feel an obligation to compel others to honor and obey such restrictions, which is why many of them become cops or judges or ministers.

I realize, being an only child myself, that I'm constrained by a sense of duty to achieve equity whenever I can. So I'm driven to find Mossler's murderer. And, perhaps, the killer of Wade Lawrence, the boy in Denver.

The minister finishes, then invites a spokesman for the family, a tall young man who's a cousin, to come up front to give some personal insights about the deceased.

Now Jeff whispers, "I contacted the other two boys in Zipdata, the ones from San Antonio and San Francisco."

"Which ones are they?"

"See the skinny redheaded kid beside David and Pete in the third row on the left? That's the one from Texas, Will Tanger. He agreed to talk with us tomorrow morning. The black kid beside him is the other one. He says he has to get back to California this afternoon."

The cousin begins speaking, telling of growing up with the Mossler kid, how they used to play tennis, how they formed a computer club at Hillsboro High, and then attended KU together. Ten minutes later, he finishes his speech. The organist starts another hymn. "What's your take on the kid from California?" I ask.

Jeff shrugs. "Only talked to him a minute. He seemed cooperative, but said he really needed to get back for a meeting."

"What's his name again?"

"Damian Roberts," Jeff says, and I tell him, "After I finish in Denver, I'll grab a flight to San Francisco. We need to talk with him pronto."

Jeff says, "I thought you might say that."

I drop off Binga at her favorite kennel. She looks underwhelmed. I shrug, then wave good-bye as she sighs and drops into a corner of the cage. Disgruntled dogs. You know?

During the drive to the Kansas City airport, I keep mulling over how Kyle Mossler died. Puncture wound in the neck. Curare.

I'm pondering the circumstance that no syringe was found. No dart. Nothing.

Falling in behind a Peterbilt tractor-trailer rig doing seventy-five, my tires humming on the interstate, I consider exotic weapons. In particular, sharp, pointed ones. The kind prison inmates and guys with criminal minds concoct.

One pertinent type might be those fashioned from a ball-point pen. The thin metal cylinder inside some pens can be cut, and a tiny flange made, producing a handcuff key. And I'm thinking the pen point could be sharpened and the cylinder filled with curare. I'll have Arty check to see if David had a pen when searched, or if one was found at the crime scene.

Then there's the other murder in Denver. Apparently done differently, but I wouldn't be surprised if the same person or persons weren't behind that killing, too. Though

73

what the motive could be still puzzles me.

I'll wait until I have a look at the details of the Lawrence kid's murder before I start drawing any comparisons or trying to link them. But the fact that these two young men died one after the other, both members of the same computer company, does make me suspicious. Plus, there's the odd manner of each of the killings.

And as I hurtle along the highway, surveying the fields with snow gleaming whitely, I get an idea which seems too exotic to have any merit. Still, there's got to be a solution to Mossler's death. And unless I explore every avenue, I have a feeling no one will find it.

It's been a calm flight from Kansas City to Denver, and now as the plane starts its descent, I study the mountains with their snowy peaks and formidable bulk. Magnificent. There's nothing quite so humbling to a mere mortal man as gazing at a mountain range.

Denver has had several days with no snow. So the Lawrence kid had gone jogging in the park in January. The man giving the weather report said a new front is headed into the Rockies in two days and will probably dump half a foot of new white stuff, then move on into the Midwest.

I'm sure the ski resort managers will be rejoicing. Snow and ice are their dear friends. Which brings to mind: Some say the world will end in fire, some say in ice.

I can't say I'm elated by either choice.

I come out of the chute with the other departing passengers, feeling that instant of dislocation I always have when I've gotten off a flight, as though I'm trying to get my sea legs. Then there's the sensation that I'm a stranger in a strange land. All these people, scurrying here and there, greeting each other with hugs and kisses and loud conversations, and not one soul looks familiar or has any idea who I am or cares if I somehow disappear in the next second.

"Austin? That you?"

Cajun accent. My head snaps to the right to take in a burly, red-faced man with hair more gray than brown, intense brown eyes tinged with the habitual drinker's red, branching road map.

"Yes . . . are you . . . ?"

"Detective Fournier, Denver PD. Thought you could use a tour guide."

I'm impressed. "That's nice of you, Detective," I say, shaking his large, rough hand. He's got a stocky man's strength. And though he'd look out of shape in a health club, I judge he'd be tough to take out in a bar fight.

"You didn't need to meet me," I add. "I was going to call you tonight."

He shrugs. "I wasn't doing nothing anyhow."

No wedding ring. Apparently no serious relationship going on. Like many in law enforcement, he probably has a divorce or two under his belt.

"Would you have time for a beer, Detective? Maybe fill me in on your case?"

"I know a fine spot, for sure, Max. The best buy is their pitchers."

"I never turn down a bargain."

After I check in at a downtown hotel, we head for a tavern. It's a huge place, with long bars, scattered tables and chairs, and pool tables and other gaming machines spread about. The joint's crowded with whooping bunches of twenty- and thirty-something-year-olds. There's also a complement of middle-aged folks, most of them looking in good physical condition, trying to stay young. I suck in my stomach and throw my shoulders back. No sense slouching.

A brunette in khaki slacks and a blue knit shirt takes our order for a pitcher of Rocky Mountain Kool-Aid and some chili burgers. Health food has its limits. And taste makes up for a lot of nutritional defects.

After Fournier quaffs half his suds in three huge gulps, he wipes his mouth, sets the chilled mug down with a thump on the wooden table, and looks me straight in the eye. "You worked any homicides before?"

I'm drinking, too, the cool elixir sliding down smoothly here in the Mile High City, but I choke, with air and brew going down the wrong pipe. Clearing my throat, I say, "Being a fed, murder cases weren't my specialty, of course. But I handled a few."

He scratches his large honker, lips pressed together, considering. "Then you solved them, you?"

I take another swallow. "Absolutely."

"That's a start." He hoists his mug, holds it out toward me, and I clunk it with mine. "Here's to another scumsucker meeting his due."

"Just too bad," I muse, "there's no swampful of gators to drop him into."

A blink. "That Cajun-speak come out my mouth, no matter how I try different."

"No problem. I like the rhythm."

He finishes his drink and grabs the pitcher to pour another. "Me, I like it, too. It's the Lou gives me fits about it. Tight-ass lady officer, you know?"

"I've dealt with some."

"But there's some other things you might like."

"Such as?"

"She fill out that shirt real good. And she's divorced two years now."

"So?"

"She might not mind keeping company with a smooth guy like you."

I finish my mug, then hold it out to him. "Keep pouring, pal."

After we dispense with the guy talk about the Lou's looks, the chitchat about what Denver has to offer, and the inevitable confession as to why Fournier left Louisiana for the high country (nasty divorce, but no kids), we get down to the details about the murder. He goes over pretty much what I'd already learned over the phone. And he hands me a copy of his reports.

"So, you see, Max, that's what we got. Not too much, huh?"

"Some cases start out slow."

"And, *mon ami,* in murder cases, they get as cold as the corpse real damn quick."

"I notice you don't have a coroner's report. Has he said anything?"

Fournier rubs his face with his hand, looking irritated. "All he says so far is 'heart attack.' Big doo-dah help, no?"

"But he's still working on it?"

"I told him he'd better find something more, or else."

"You're saying you intimidated him?"

"I didn't say nothing more than that, but he prob'ly think I gonna squeeze his bony head like a crawfish until it pop off."

I suppress a chuckle. "So I suppose he's hard at it?"

Fournier takes another gulp, sets down his mug, his ruddy face darkening, and says, "You can damn well bet on it."

I finish my beer and say I'd better turn in. I don't mention that I have some homework to finish. During the flight, I found some interesting facts in two books I bought about poisons.

Chapter 9

All comfy in my briefs and T-shirt, propped up on pillows on the motel bed, I'm reading about the substances man has discovered or devised over the years to rid himself of other annoying or threatening humans. I'm reminded of a quote by Jean Paul Sartre: "Hell is other people." Hard to dispute the guy.

So laws have been passed to force our tolerance of others, including the restraint from killing even those who probably deserve it. I'm reading descriptions of the effects of poisons on the body. I soon realize it would be a horrible way to go.

Poisons can cause symptoms such as vomiting, convulsions, nausea, blurred vision, paralysis, unconsciousness, and death.

I'd much rather be conked on the bean with a meteorite.

But do I even have evidence that the Lawrence kid was poisoned? No, there's just the description of a man holding something up to his face, then him keeling over. But since Mossler was poisoned, I've got a hunch Lawrence might have been, too.

The section on curare in one of the books matches what the coroner told me about Mossler's death and the symptoms he displayed. What I need to locate now is a different kind of poison that can simulate death by heart attack. No piece of cake.

The police reports furnish statements by the female jogger and the EMTs who treated Lawrence at the park; they indicate he died suddenly. So, supposing the man who ran up to him and stuck something in his face was the one who killed him, the killer would've used a fast-acting poison, probably dispensed as a liquid or vapor. Something that'd bring on a cardiac arrest, or what looked like one.

The old standby arsenic doesn't seem to fit. Although it can be dispensed as a gas called arsine, it's usually found as arsenic trioxide, which is a white powder. The effects include gastric distress and vomiting, with convulsions and a coma to follow.

Similarly, strychnine can be inhaled, but it causes severe muscle spasms and convulsions, leaving the victim arched backward, with rigor mortis setting in immediately. Swell. Makes me want to carry my pistol wherever I go. Not that I'm in any danger. Unless, of course, I choose to believe the veiled threat on my message machine.

But ignoring that possibility for now, I continue to leaf through pages, trying to find, as I assume the killer did, the perfect poison for this situation. Monkshood and wolfbane are poisonous plants which cause paralysis, chest pain, and a weak pulse. The heart muscle becomes paralyzed. But it's usually ingested or absorbed through the skin, unless the murderer figured a way to make a liquid or gaseous solution.

Extracts or the sap of oleander cause respiratory paralysis. They also stimulate the heart, then cause sweating, unconsciousness, and death almost immediately. They seem like good candidates.

Taxine, an extract of the English yew tree, causes shock, coma, and cardiac failure. Usually within an hour. Would it be quicker if inhaled or squirted into the mouth or eyes?

The notes in my binder are piling up. I'm pretty sure the coroner won't like testing for all these possibilities (all right, they're guesses), but I don't know what else to pursue. "If it wasn't some kind of poison," I ask my mirrored reflection across the room, "what could it be?"

My image remains as close-mouthed and still as I am, so I return to my reading.

Foxglove is an herb which can cause blurred vision, an irregular pulse rate, and death by ventricular fibrillation. But it takes twenty minutes or so. As I feared, the list seems to be growing, but I'm not sure I've found a substance which would fulfill all the criteria of Lawrence's death.

Wait a minute. Here's ipecac, a plant whose berries and juice are both deadly. But I thought that was used to combat poisoning.

Ah, and so it is, I see. But an overdose can cause unconsciousness, collapse, and death from heart failure. And it can take effect immediately.

Hey. I may be onto it. Sure sounds strong.

But wait, it says here it's usually administered orally or by injection. So I'll have to check with the coroner about any puncture marks. And this may help, too: an autopsy should show degeneration of the kidneys, liver, and heart. Something that shouldn't show up in a young man.

I stand up and pace about the room, thinking. Tomorrow I have to talk with the coroner, and also try to interview the young woman who witnessed the death. Maybe it wouldn't hurt to talk to the EMTs, either.

When I'm nervous or eager to do something, but have to wait, I try to work off a little energy. So I hit the floor and do some push-ups. Then I roll over and go into a crunch routine, cutting up my upper and lower abs, which I know must be somewhere under that little roll of fat.

That done, I use a rubber stretch exerciser to tone my upper body; I'll have to work the lower half by doing a lot of walking tomorrow. Breathing stronger, with fresh blood and oxygen pumping to my brain, I notice it's getting late, so I sit down beside the phone and call Amy. She picks up on the fourth ring, sounding sleepy.

"Oh, sorry, it sounds like I woke you."

"Max? I dropped off about an hour ago. I thought midnight sort of signaled the end of the day."

Oops. I forgot it's an hour later there.

"Anyway," she says, "I called you a couple of times earlier, but you were out."

Guess I forgot to tell her I was traveling. So I tell her.

"You flew to *Denver?*"

"Sorry, I probably should have called you before I left."

"I see."

She sounds disappointed, much like a schoolteacher who's been let down. "But I should be back in a couple of days. I just have to check out some things here, then fly to San Francisco for an interview."

"What's going on?"

I run it down for her.

"Hmmm," she remarks, not sounding too impressed. "Do you want me to feed Binga while you're gone?"

"Thanks, but I put her in a kennel."

"I thought she didn't like it there."

"She's hard to please. But I do the best I can."

"Well, that's good training for you, anyway."

"I don't plan on having any more pets."

"That's not what I meant."

"So," I say, "how are things with David and Jeff?" Not a graceful segue, but she assures me they're fine. She adds that maybe the worst is past for them.

I hope she's right. And I hope they're not in danger. I wonder if I should tell her about my poison theory?

"I'm guessing you're thinking about something."

She's got me there. "I'm working on a hypothesis. It may be pretty far out."

She sighs. She's used to the way I work. So I explain it.

"But that sounds . . ."

For a moment, she's at a loss for words.

"Wild?" I say.

"Crazy. Are you thinking these murders are connected? That there's some conspiracy involved?"

"You know I don't usually believe in conspiracies, but in this case, I feel I have to check it out."

"But who could possibly want to kill these kids? And why?"

"Well, there you go. Those are the questions that've been haunting me."

"No wonder you can't sleep."

"I'm going down for the count soon. I just need to do a little more research."

"I've got a hearing tomorrow, so I'd better go. But as the attorney for David, I must insist you keep me apprised of your whereabouts and actions."

"But I'm the world's most inscrutable detective."

"So I've heard you say, but I'm the world's nosiest barrister."

"No one's perfect, so get back to sleep, and have sweet dreams."

A barely audible sigh. "You, too. And keep in touch."

"Yes, Mom." I hang up, then pick up one of the books, determined to plow through to the end. Or slip into a coma trying.

Henbane, a plant whose juice is deadly, works in fifteen minutes on the central nervous system. Procaine and Lidocaine are colorless liquids which can immediately cause coma and cardiac arrest, but are usually injected. Percodan can be given by injection or orally and can produce a coma and cardiac arrest within thirty minutes.

All righty, then. Epinephrine can be given by inhalation, producing immediate cardiac arrhythmia, coma, and respiratory failure. Chloramine-T can be inhaled, causing collapse, respiratory failure, and quick death.

Now I'm getting the feeling that only the coroner will be able to sort all this out. Here's another possibility: Benzene, a colorless liquid which can also become a vapor, could certainly do the trick. Upon inhalation, the vic experiences dizziness, cardiac palpitations, tightness in the chest, paralysis, unconsciousness, and, possibly, a heart attack. Wow.

Odds sure seem to be in favor of a killer who knows about poisons. Of course, an autopsy can detect most of these substances. But then, there would have to be the suspicion that the death wasn't a simple cardiac arrest. And even if the cause of death were identified as a particular poison, especially one which is widely available, a connection would have to be found between the killer and the victim. The old game of "Who has the motive?" And the opportunity.

Plunging ahead, I see that hydrogen sulfide, a gas which can be inhaled, could cause an immediate coma and rapid death. But there's the telltale smell of rotten eggs, like when there's a leak in a natural gas line. My guess is this wasn't used. But, hey, I've been wrong a couple of times during my career.

Of course, there are also a number of street drugs which can cause death by overdose or hypersensitivity to them, but as I skim the effects of the various ones, none seems to quite fit the circumstances of Lawrence's death as I know it to this point. So, I flip back through the book once more. And, sure enough, here's something I missed.

Cyanide seems to fit the bill. In liquid or gaseous form, it acts immediately, causing unconsciousness and convulsions. Death can occur within a minute or so. At first I skipped by it, because both potassium cyanide and sodium cyanide are solids with the old almond smell.

But reading further, I see that hydrogen cyanide is a deadly gas. Used by the Nazis in their horror chambers in World War II death camps. Also currently used in our country by several states to execute criminals.

Memory serving, Timothy McVeigh, one of the Oklahoma City bombers, was executed at Terre Haute by use of potassium chloride—a heart-stopping drug. But it was injected. Every time I recall McVeigh, it gives me pause, as he was the only criminal that I personally identified during my FBI career who was put to death. Still, because he was responsible for 168 deaths in the blast, I thought he deserved it.

Back to the books, I see that prussic acid was thought to have been used by Lizzie Borden on her parents, not content with merely mauling them with her trusty ax.

Prussic acid was also used by Russian hit men in 1957. They had a metal tube of the stuff with a firing device that sprayed the poison into their quarry's face. Blood vessels constricted immediately, death resembled a heart attack, and relaxation after death hid the evidence.

And it was used in another assassination in 1958, but tiny slivers of glass were found in the victim's face, as the killers apparently used a test tube or a similar delivery system.

An interesting note in one of the books suggests that such a poison could be delivered by an air gun shooting a dart. Hardly any noise. Accurate at a moderate distance.

Damn. Maybe a small dart could've been shot at Mossler. But, once again, where the heck did it go? Could Sanders have been in on the hit? Maybe he picked up the dart before anyone noticed it, even before anyone arrived on the scene. Then destroyed it?

Maybe it's still somewhere in his house or around the premises. But I'd be hard-pressed to come up with valid probable cause to put in a request for a search warrant. This is way too speculative.

I close the book and sigh, then pile the tomes on the nightstand. Washing my face and brushing my teeth makes me feel somewhat cleansed, and I jump under the covers and switch off the light. But as I try to drop off to sleep, visions of darts, test tubes, and deadly substances keep whirling through my mind. It's quite a far-flung galaxy of death. Completely lethal to anyone who interferes with the killers.

Chapter 10

Morning comes early here in the mountains. I suck in a mouthful of Denver air, stretch, then open one eye. It stings. Probably bloodshot from lack of sleep and too many brewskys. But there's no time for whining, I'm here on an important mission.

So I roll out, take a long shower, shave, and jump into my jeans and sports coat, ready to fight the world of crime. But first I search out the hotel dining room to fortify myself with some eggs and toast. As I review the *Denver Post* and watch people gulping their coffee, I also down some milk and orange juice, hoping to replace some of the bad fluids gurgling through my veins.

By the time I arrive at the Denver PD, the latent werewolf in me has subsided. I'm feeling close to human. Or at least a viable subspecies thereof.

Detective Fournier comes to the front desk to greet me, takes one look, and says, "Damn, you look raggedy this morning."

"Nice to see you, too, Detective. I'm not accustomed to the altitude."

"Yeah, them mile-high hangovers are a bad news bitch."

We pace back to the squad room. Standing in the middle of a group of detectives is the most striking redhead I've ever seen. I nudge Fournier, saying, "She's not—"

But then she turns her gaze toward us and smiles. Dazzling. The crisp white blouse and dark blue skirt curve in every feminine way.

"Lou," Fournier says as we approach, "here's the wonder boy from the flatlands. All set to help out us bumbling mountain folks."

"Not at all, Lieutenant Bartles," I say, reading her nametag as I hold out my hand, "I'm just hoping to collaborate with you."

She chuckles as she takes my hand, and I realize I'm on the embarrassing end of a double entendre. "We might be able to work something out, Mr. Austin."

The gaggle of detectives grin bigtime.

My ears are burning red. This isn't like me. I'm the cool private detective. Inscrutable. Unflappable.

"Just call me Max. If you'd like, we can step into your office and compare what we've got."

She glances around at the others, obviously enjoying the moment.

"You mean," she says, "you'll show me yours if I show you mine?"

"That about covers it. Although I'll get the better of that deal." I give her the once-over, thinking that the best defense is a good offense.

Now she pinks up a little. Which does nothing to diffuse her beauty. Women have it easy in the skirmish between the sexes. "We'll see about that. I'm ready if you are. Gabe, you want to come along and watch the show?"

"No way I'd miss a good gator wrassling, Lieutenant. I'm right behind you."

So we march into her glassed-in office. I'm rapidly revising my preconceptions of the tough female types who advance in law enforcement. This lady is all class.

She settles behind a large wooden desk. Crossing one long

leg over the other, she opens a folder that's laid out before her. She puts a hand atop the papers, asking, "Did Gabe give you copies of our reports?"

I pat my binder. "Got 'em right here. Interesting case."

"And you think it fits with yours?"

She's being serious, I think. So I play it straight, saying, "Looks suspicious to me, Lieutenant. Both young men belong to a small company, both seem to have died under strange circumstances."

"Call me Karen. Gabe said your vic was poisoned?"

"Curare. Delivered by injection. Maybe a dart or syringe."

"You don't know how it happened?"

"The murder weapon wasn't found."

"Anyway," she says, waving a hand, "we don't have any evidence that our case was a murder. Coroner says heart attack."

"But you've got the guy coming up to him from the woods, then running off."

"According to a young woman at the park." There's a trace of doubt in her voice.

"Don't you believe her, Karen?"

She cuts Fournier a glance, and there's a sudden heaviness to the thin air. He shifts in his seat, then says, "I believe she thinks she saw what she told us." He frowns, then continues, "But there's some flies in the gumbo."

"What's that mean?"

The lieutenant lets out a breath between pursed lips. "She's not the perfect witness. She's got problems."

"She's slow," Fournier says.

I'm waiting.

He touches the side of his head. "Upstairs, you know. Not exactly retarded, but within spittin' distance."

"But she saw what she saw."

The lieutenant studies the ceiling.

Fournier waggles a hand. "Maybe so. But she was real upset, and, like I'm telling you, she don't take in all the subtle moments of life."

"Could I talk with her?"

The lieutenant nods. Her eyes are as green as sparkly emeralds. "We've got no problem with that. But don't expect too much. I think we got everything she had. Besides, we don't want to put any ideas in her head."

"I understand, Karen. I just want to get an impression of her and what she saw. I won't make any suggestions to her."

She gives me a half smile, which beats most women going all out. "Anything else we can do for you?"

"I'd like to see the crime scene. Then I want to talk with the coroner about some possibilities."

"Such as?" She recrosses her legs. Runs a hand over her nylons.

I give her a rundown on what I read last night.

"So you're strong on the poison angle?"

"I think it's worth checking."

"No big thing," says Fournier. "Let's go see that little park, then we'll pass by and gab with the death dabbler."

"I'll go, too," says the lieutenant. "I like seeing great minds at work."

"You're setting yourself up for a big disappointment," I say.

She shrugs into her jacket. I see no way she could button it. "We'll see."

Low in the sky, the Sun glares over the park's edge, throwing tree shadows across the wood chip path like black fingers grasping for unsuspecting passersby. A cool breeze brushes through as we study the surroundings. In the last ten minutes, only two joggers have pounded past our small assemblage of crime fighters.

"Not a lot of foot traffic," I say.

Fournier shrugs. "Lots of kids are in the mountains now. They're skiing or snowboarding. Chasing nookie in the lodges."

Lieutenant Bartles ignores him.

"This is about the spot where the boy fell, isn't it, Gabe?" she asks.

He picks up a stick and points at a spot on the path. "Right here. He was running in that direction," he says, thumbing back over his shoulder.

"And the young woman came from around that bend?" I ask.

He turns his head to take a peek, then nods.

Bartles points toward the bushes and trees to our left. "The mystery guy came out of there, according to the witness."

Thirty feet from the path, I'd say. Pretty dense cover, even in winter. As I walk toward the brush, with Fournier and Bartles following, I hear the screech of tires on pavement not far away.

There's just a trace of a path, seldom used, I'd imagine. Still, I follow it into the trees, noting a scuff mark that looks pretty fresh. We duck branches and shuffle through undergrowth for about forty feet, then emerge by the street, with traffic churning past.

There's a turn-in at the edge of the park, close by. Two or three cars could squeeze in there. I look down the street, noting there are a couple more short parking strips. Maybe—

"Could have been a car waiting here," says Bartles.

I gaze into her eyes, suddenly losing my train of thought. "Let's check around a bit," I say.

And we do, walking along the edge of the space, staring at the ground as if we've lost a contact lens. At first we see nothing. Then over by the tree line a few feet away I spot a small, crumpled brown paper sack. So much for protecting the environment.

I pull gloves from my jacket pocket, tug them on, then pick up the sack. There's some heft to the bag; something's in it. I open it carefully.

"What you got?" asks Fournier.

"Apple core," I say.

"Baltimore," says Bartles.

"So, who be your friend?" Fournier says, a grin across his face.

We look at her, and she shrugs it off, so we all turn our attention to the healthy snack. Red Delicious is my guess. Eaten down pretty clean.

I check the bottom of the sack. There's a receipt from a grocery store. For an apple and a pack of cigarettes.

"That store's a couple of blocks from here," says Fournier. "It's a big chain."

Lots of customers going through, we're all thinking.

I read the receipt more carefully. "Purchased at six-fifty a.m., two days ago," I say.

Now the lieutenant is interested. "About an hour before the murder."

Now she thinks it's a murder.

"Gabe," she says, "you'd better ask them about it."

He shrugs, but pulls out some plastic bags, and I drop the evidence into various ones.

We check the ground more deliberately. Sure enough, I spot a cigarette butt lying there, not squashed out, just left to burn down. Maybe dropped from a parked car? Driver's side, I'd say. It proves to be a Kool, same brand noted on the receipt. Filter tip. Long.

Fournier holds out another small plastic bag.

"What's that?" asks Bartles, pointing at the ground.

A slim pamphlet of some sort, dirty, like it's been run over. I pick it up. It's a map of the Denver area. From Avis Rent-a-Car.

Her hair brushes against my arm as she peeks over my shoulder. "What are you thinking?"

I guess she means what *was* I thinking. "That this might've been dropped by someone in a hurry."

"Maybe a hightailing scoundrel?" says Fournier.

"I doubt this park's a big tourist attraction." I make a mental note of the address stamped on the map, then hand it over.

"Nothing attached to it about a specific rental car?" Bartles asks.

"No, it's just the map," I admit.

Fournier frowns. "The witness didn't see the guy get into a vehicle. We've got no idea what kind of car to look for."

I shrug. "A man renting anything a day or two before the murder."

I'm thinking of how the FBI reviewed half a million passports in the Martin Luther King assassination case. Grunt work, however tedious, can pay off.

"According to the stamp on that pamphlet," says Bartles, "it came from the airport. I'm sure they rented a ton of cars in two days."

"We could get a list of the renters' names," I offer. "In case any of them come up again in our investigation."

Fournier peers at the various items in the clear plastic bags. "I'll see if we can get latents off any of the papers."

Bartles turns away, checking the rest of the area.

I look around some more myself. From the far end of the

parking area I look back, able to see a portion of the jogging path.

Bartles stops, turns, and puts her hands on her hips. "That seems to be everything. I don't see any tire tracks."

I glance at her, then Fournier. "That's it for me," I say.

"Anyone for lunch?" she asks.

"I've got a sandwich at the office, so I'll pass," says Fournier. "And I'll talk to the cashier at the grocery store, then get these things to the lab."

"I'm up for some chow," I say. "Better now than after we see the coroner."

Chapter 11

After lunch at a great deli, Lieutenant Bartles and I head to the coroner's office, with her wheeling through busy traffic and with me buckled in tight and gripping the seat.

"Does my driving make you nervous?" she says.

I think I detect a grin.

"Karen, I'm the world's most fearless P.I.," I say. "However, truth be told, there *are* some things about you that scare me."

"Why, Max. Whatever do you mean by that?"

"Let's just say you're . . . intimidating. Beautiful, brainy, and beguiling. And with great table manners—for a cop."

"I like the way you handle yourself, too." She changes lanes abruptly, then accelerates hard, passing an old truck that's chugging out a stream of blue exhaust.

"Jerk," she comments. Then, settling back to seventy, says, "Are you married, divorced, separated?"

"Widowed. About a year and a half ago."

"Not involved with anyone?"

"Just my dog, and it's strictly platonic."

"Then it's too bad I've given up on men. And that you live so far away."

I'm at a momentary loss.

She laughs. "Just giving you a hard time. All right, I do think most men are creeps, but you haven't set off my warning meter. Yet."

"Give me time," I say.

"I just may," she says, looking me up and down.

"Bus!" I yell.

She hits the brakes and swerves right, nearly clipping the rear of the looming silver behemoth. "I was going to take this next exit, anyway."

She's cool as a mountain breeze.

I'm shaking like an aspen in a snowstorm.

By the time we get to the coroner's office, I've managed to compose myself. In fact, I'm pretty much back in charge of the world. Bartles introduces me to a short, bald man with wrinkled pants, bags under his eyes, and black horn-rim glasses perched halfway down his nose.

We shake, with me wondering where his clammy hands have been lately.

"Do you feel all right, Mr. Austin?" he asks. "You look pale."

"Probably the thin mountain air," I say.

Bartles chuckles to herself. "Or the hairpin turns."

"Sit, sit," he says, and we take chairs in his smallish office. "What can I do for you, Officers?"

I ask to see the photographs from the autopsy. Bartles and I look them over, then I spend the next five minutes telling him about the poison killing in Kansas and what I suspect may have happened to the jogger here.

"I didn't get anything on our tox screen," he says.

"Then my best guess would be he used prussic acid," I say. "The vapor would dissipate quickly. It'd look like a heart attack."

With his mouth screwed up, his eyes squinting, he says, "That's possible."

Like he was agreeing that I may have spotted a UFO in the parking lot.

"This photo," I say, holding it out toward him.

"Yes?" He takes it in hand and glances at it, then looks back at me.

"There are red spots on his face. Let's say the attacker used a glass tube to dispense the vapor. The accelerating charge might have splintered the glass, and there could be minuscule slivers in his flesh."

He pushes his glasses up and studies the photo more carefully. "I recall that I thought those were probably tiny scrapes or abrasions from his collapsing onto the ground."

"It was a wood chip path. Pretty soft."

Now Lieutenant Bartles is leaning forward, listening intently.

"I see what you're saying," he agrees, "but I don't know if—"

"Can you check that out, Jacob?" Bartles asks. "We'd like to know for sure."

He gestures, flipping his wrist back, palm up. "Of course, Lieutenant. No problem. I've got a couple of other matters to handle right now, but I'll call you later."

We get up, thank him, then leave.

It's exhilarating to get back out into the fresh air.

"Do you think he'll find anything, Max?"

"Heck if I know, but we could sure use a break."

"If this was a stranger killing," she says, "that's exactly what we need."

But I think there must be some link between the killings. I may know more after I talk with the witness. I could use a good mile-high miracle.

Lieutenant Bartles drives back to the PD. She has business to handle. I pick up my rental car and get directions to the address where the witness lives. It takes me a half hour, but I finally find her small house on a quiet residential street not far from the park.

A middle-aged woman with gray, curly hair and a faded dress opens the door. She has the facial wrinkles of the continually worried. But she's pleasant, and when I identify myself, she invites me in.

The living room is dark for such a sunny day. No fresh breezes coming through open doors or windows. Heavy curtains at every portal. The type of place where people get depressed and commit suicide. Peachy.

"Is Jennifer home?" I ask.

She sighs. "Yes, she's in her room. But is it necessary to talk with her? I mean, she was very upset when that boy collapsed, and then the police wanted to talk with her, and all. She's rather . . . shy around people. I don't want her getting distraught again."

"I understand perfectly. I promise I'll be brief, and I won't push her. You can stay in the room with us if you wish." Usually, I don't approve of having outside influences, but it's better than not getting to talk with the girl at all.

"All right, I'll get her. It'll be a minute or so."

"No hurry."

In a few minutes, Mrs. Jenkins returns, motioning Jennifer to follow.

Jennifer must be twenty or so, but she exudes a younger presence; she has the look of a frightened rabbit, and with her soft brown hair, full cheeks, and rounded figure, she projects the same timidity. She perches rigidly on the edge of a chair. I immediately want to protect her, to shield her from any unpleasantness.

But I have a job to do. "Jennifer, my name's Max. I'm an investigator, and I'm looking into what happened to that boy in the park the other day."

Her eyes glint with interest. "Is that Camry your police car?"

So she's been watching. "No, it's one I rented. I flew here from Kansas."

"Oh." She seems to retreat back into some private world.

"But I drive a Trailblazer to do my work there."

She nods. "That's cool," she says, appraisingly.

"Could I talk to you about what you saw in the park?"

She nods again, but looks toward the kitchen as if she'd rather be anywhere else in the Universe.

"That's a pretty park you were in. Do you go there often?"

She turns her head toward me, a bunny sniffing the air. "I like to walk around there and see the squirrels play."

"I watch the squirrels at my place in Kansas," I say. "Did you ever see them in the tops of trees, jumping from one branch to another? Sometimes, they slip and have to hang on for dear life."

She giggles. She must have seen them. "They look like those people at the circus."

"The ones on the flying trapeze? I hadn't thought of that, but they really do."

I glance at her mother. She doesn't look as tense as before. Even gives a slight smile.

"I talked with the police, Jennifer. They said you saw the young man who got hurt at the park."

Her expression goes taut.

"I just want to help him and his family," I tell her.

She fidgets with her hands. Bright orange fingernail polish that she must've applied herself. She's staring at her lap.

But she starts to talk. "I'm . . . not sure what happened. A man ran up to him, and then he just stopped jogging. He fell down and laid real still."

"Did the man do something to him?"

She frowns, struggling to remember. "He stuck his hand up to the boy's face. Then there was a pop."

"A pop?"

She's staring at me, eyes wide. "Like a light bulb. Flashes, then pops. When it burns out, you know?"

I nod. "Of course. Then what happened?"

"The boy fell down, and the man ran back into the trees."

"Was the man bigger or smaller than I am?"

She regards me. "Could you stand up?"

"Sure." I do, and she backs off a couple of paces, then looks me over.

"He was a little shorter than you. But slimmer."

"Dark or light hair?"

Just then the phone rings in the kitchen, and Jennifer jumps, her head turning sharply toward the sound.

"We'll let the machine get it," says her mother. "Go ahead, dear."

"Uh, I think his hair was dark. He had on a black suit, and his skin looked real white. No tan."

"Older or younger than I am?"

"Maybe younger. A little."

"Do you remember his face?"

"No, I . . . I don't."

Her mother clears her throat, and I glance at her. It's a signal to wrap it up. But I've gotten nowhere.

So I wing a last attempt. "Did the car make a lot of noise when it left?"

"I don't know. Maybe. I just went over to the boy."

She's fidgeting, averting her eyes. I sense she's fibbing. "I know, honey. But did you hear or see the car leave?"

"I looked at him real close. His skin was getting sorta gray."

"But then—"

"Then he got awful still. I was real scared." She's staring at the carpet. "The police asked me a lot of questions. It was hard to remember all of what happened."

Her lips are pressed together tightly, and she's working at her hands like crazy.

"So you forgot to tell them you saw the car drive off?"

"I didn't forget. I just wasn't sure what kind it was. I didn't want to say anything wrong."

"But when you heard it pull away, you looked up and saw the car through the trees, didn't you?"

Head down, looking miserable, she nods slowly.

"Was the man in it?"

"I think it was him. And there was another man."

"What did the car look like?"

"I didn't see it too good. I don't know for sure if it was last year's or this year's Taurus. They look a lot alike."

"A Ford Taurus? Are you sure about that?" I shoot a look at her mother.

"Jennifer's always been fascinated by cars. Even before . . ." She hesitates.

"I didn't mean to—"

"It's all right," she says. "Jennifer fell from a tree when she was ten. She got a bad head injury. It's been . . . hard for us all."

I wait. She sniffs, then looks up at me. "She watches all the car shows on TV, and sometimes I buy her auto magazines at the grocery store. It seems to keep her interested and somewhat alert."

I turn back to Jennifer. "You've been a big help, dear. Thanks for remembering so much for me."

She brightens a bit. "You want my best guess?"

I smile at her and nod. "You bet, Jennifer."

"I think it was a new one. Dark blue, four-door, XL package. With a Colorado tag."

Chapter 12

Back at the coroner's office, I'm waiting in the hallway to see the elf in baggy pants. He opens his office door and beckons me in, and I notice his face is flushed, with wrinkles of concern grooving his forehead. Maybe he saw a ghost.

"Yes, Mr. Austin, can I help you?"

"I'm leaving town, and I wondered if you'd checked the red spots on the Lawrence kid's face."

Clouds seem to gather behind his eyes.

"Sit, sit," he says. He fiddles with some papers on his desk. "Yes, I did. They appeared to be scrapes of some kind. Probably recent, but I seriously doubt they were connected to the death."

"No glass slivers?"

"Nothing that I saw. I'm sorry. There just wasn't anything to confirm your suspicions."

He waits a beat, then says, "So if that's everything, I've got an appointment." He stands.

I stand, nonplussed, then shake his hand and thank him.

As I'm walking down the hallway, confusion fogging my brain, a conjecture coalesces into a clear thought: Liar, liar, baggy pants on fire. His hand was damp, his voice strained, and his eyes had the rabbit look, like Jennifer got when I asked her about the car.

But what the hell reason would he have to cover something up?

★ ★ ★ ★ ★

The glamorous Lieutenant Bartles is tied up in a meeting in her office, but Detective Fournier is available—my luck.

"Come on in, cowboy. Drag up a tumbleweed and sit a spell, you."

"Now you're getting in tune with the real world, partner."

He shrugs. "Since I left crawfish heaven, nothing seems too sensible no more, you hear?"

"For sure, that," I acknowledge.

"Anyway, I checked the grocery store, *mon ami,* and the clerk didn't remember nothing about whoever bought the apple and ciggies. They're pretty busy that time of morning, them."

"Naturally."

So I tell him what the coroner said, and about my reservations.

He frowns, shaking his head. "Old Jacob's weird as a hairless dog. We've mostly got used to it. Don't know you can read anything into him being nervous and all. Maybe you just intimidated him."

I don't think I usually do that. "It just seems odd." I start to tell him what Jennifer said about the popping noise, but for some reason I hesitate.

"You talk with that girl?" he asks, reading my transparent mind.

So I tell him about Jennifer identifying the car.

He mulls it over. "That's real good, Max, if she ain't just imagining she saw it to make you happy."

"I think she really saw it. And she seems to know cars."

"Speaking of which, I also passed by the airport and caged a rental car list."

"Could I get a copy?"

"Sure, I'll make you one. But just let me look . . ." he says, pulling a computer printout from his desk drawer. "Here we go. You say she thought she saw a Ford Taurus?"

"Probably new, most rentals are, and it may be dark blue, four-door."

"Umm hmmm," he intones absently, scanning the printout. He flips to the next page. Starts shaking his head. "Nope, no sir, I don't see nothing like that. At least not during this two-day list I've got." He looks up at me and tilts his head sympathetically.

"Damn, I thought we might have a line on something."

He shrugs, then puts the list away. "Hard to tell, with that girl, what she saw, and what she didn't."

I have a different take, but there's no sense arguing a moot point.

"I'd better get out to the airport," I say. "My flight's in a couple of hours." I close my binder and shake his hand. "Thanks for your patience with an outsider."

"No, no, we were glad to have your take on things. I'll let you know if we get lucky and stumble across anything else. But, straight up and real, with the coroner's report, this dog will prob'ly die a natural death."

"I understand." Not really. I glance toward Karen's office; the door's still closed. "Tell the lieutenant I had to leave, but I'll call her later."

He grins. "Thought you might. Have a good flight, you."

I drop my rental car at the Budget lot. Inside the terminal I get my boarding pass. Now, with over an hour until my flight to San Francisco, I mull over the case. Or cases. Something's niggling at the back of my consciousness. The coroner. Maybe Fournier? I have a feeling something's not on the up-and-up.

Then I sigh. I can't discern anything concrete. Guess I'll

let my subconscious chew on it awhile.

But as I walk past the car rental booths, it occurs to me I forgot to get a copy of the rental sheet from Fournier. I like to keep a complete file of all investigation in whatever case I'm working. So, stopping at the counter, I speak with a short, thick woman with shiny black hair and a dusky face showing traces of Mayan ancestry.

Luckily, she was the one who gave Fournier the list, so there's no problem with my P.I. creds. I ask for a list of rentals for three days prior to the murder. Just to get an extra shot.

She prints out the list without complaint. Service with a smile. It's becoming a rarity, but nice to see.

I thank her, stuff the list into my case, and head for the terminal for my next phase in this quest. I haven't been to San Francisco for a few years, so I'm looking forward to it, though I won't have much time to enjoy the sights. Maybe Amy would like to visit there with me when this case is over. Or possibly Lieutenant Bartles. Love, or something like it, can get so confusing.

I made it through security without suffering a strip search, so now I'm seated in the waiting area, fingering my boarding pass, and staring out the large glass windows in the terminal. Several planes roll up to the loading gates while baggage motorcarts whip around like disjointed anacondas, and some winged monsters settle onto the tarmac, while others lift skyward. One plane becomes a dot in the blue, then vanishes, and I try to peer farther into the atmosphere.

I'm reminded of Redshift 5.8 Quasar, a mere speck in the constellation Sextans, which some astronomers glimpsed and recognized to be a quasar whose light has been traveling toward us for twelve billion years. Since light travels 186,000 miles per second, that makes it a far piece off. And almost as old as the Universe.

It flits through my mind that those who fail to study history are doomed to repeat the mistakes of the past. Or something like that. And it's true; everything is affected by things that happened previously.

So it might be with my case. I've been trying to trace what happened a few days prior to the murders of Kyle Mossler and Wade Lawrence. But the precipitating factors might have occurred long before.

Maybe I should go back to when the young men first formed their company. Try to determine what the business niche was for Zipdata, and look up the kids' main customers and contacts in the business world. Couldn't hurt. Right now, I could use some more avenues to pursue. I feel as if I'm circling a roundabout, not knowing where to exit.

I glance at my case. My binder with photos, notes, etc., is inside. Also the computer list of rental vehicles. I'll check to see if I come up with anything on the extra day's list.

A heavyset man in a wrinkled blue suit plops down beside me. I nod and smile, and he wheezes a hello. Then he wrestles with a large briefcase and a carry-on suitcase.

I study the list for a bit. Hmmm, over halfway through, with no hits on the Ford Taurus. My heart is growing heavy.

And that's it. I've checked every rental for that day, and nothing matches. Maybe I should have asked for a week's list. But that would have preceded the murder of Kyle Mossler. Still, Jennifer seemed so sure.

People are getting up and forming a ragged line near the entrance to the boarding ramp. We'll be loading soon. Just for the heck of it, I continue to skim the list for the two days that Fournier already checked.

Shit. Everyone makes mistakes. So is this one?

Two days ago, a four-door Ford Taurus was rented to a

guy using a credit card and giving an address in Washington, D.C. The color might be on here somewhere, but I can't decipher the codes. Anyway, how did Fournier miss it?

I glance out the window. A plane has materialized at the gate. And at the ramp, I see the departing passengers coming out of the chute like a pack of greyhounds after a rabbit.

I grab my stuff and hustle out through the security gate, then set off with my version of an all-out sprint down the long hall. Within a few minutes, I arrive at the Avis rental counter. The Latina is helping a young black guy who looks like a power guard in the NBA.

I flash my badge at him, saying, "Airport security. We have an emergency."

The woman recognizes me and flashes a tolerant smile. "Yes, sir, what is it?"

I point at the entry on the computer printout. "Can you tell me what color this vehicle is?"

She glances at the sheet, then consults a card folder on the desk.

"Hey, man, what kinda emergency you talkin' about?" says the tall guy.

"Sorry," I say, "this will just take a second. It's very important."

"Like life or death, maybe? 'Cause it better be, I'm in a hurry—"

"It's midnight blue," she says, holding the card.

"When's it due back?"

"Listen, I got to meet some friends, you can wait 'til I get my ride." He pushes my shoulder with a large hand, moving me over a couple of feet.

"I'll finish you up right away, sir," she says.

I start to reach for his hand, maybe bend one of those long fingers back a bit, should be enough leverage to sit him down pretty quick. But I don't want to cause a scene. And I don't have much time.

She looks down at his paperwork, says, "You just need to sign here, and initial those two boxes," pointing a long fingernail with blue polish.

He shoots me a glance, then bends down to sign.

She checks her computer. "It was brought back about two hours ago," she says. "And I deal with a lot of people here. I don't remember anything about this particular rental."

Answers that question. I smile at her, then pat the guy on the back. "Thanks for your patience, sir. You may have saved someone's life."

He looks around at me and grunts. "Maybe yours, dude." Then he turns back to the form.

I wink at the pleasant woman, saying, "My lucky day."

I jog away, not because I fear bodily harm, but because I figure I've got five minutes to make my plane. In a mere four ticks of the old minute hand, I arrive panting at the ramp entrance. A curly-haired woman in a suit is glancing around the waiting area, looking ready to retreat into the bowels of the plane.

Breathless and sweating, I wave my boarding pass at her.

"You just about didn't make it," she says, appraising me with an air of disapproval.

"Story of my life," I say.

She fails to comment. Takes the boarding pass. Turns her back to me and strides along the carpeted tunnel.

Story of my life.

Chapter 13

During the flight to San Francisco, I mentally review the twisted situation. It seems that all the potentially interrelated occurrences just keep flying further apart at an accelerating pace, just as our Universe continues doing. But in every crime I've ever seen, there's some order, even if it appears to be the jumbled pattern of chaos.

If I could find a point of reference, say like the Sun in our Solar System around which all the planets coordinate their activities, then maybe I'd understand the mechanics of these criminal acts. The big question, of course, is whether some person or entity would be killing these young men, followed closely by the query: If so, who are they, and why are they doing it? Then I'll have to concoct a plan to take them down.

The plane has started its descent, with my obese seatmate doing some loud power snoring. He's missing a superb view of the city, and I wonder if I should wake him. But he looks so blissful, his mind probably soaring in dreams in a way his unwieldy body never could, and I decide against it.

So I glance back to the heavens. Whatever stars may be twinkling above San Francisco tonight are overpowered by the millions of white lights sparkling across this placid domain by the bay. If I had to live in a city, this would be one of the few I'd find palatable.

Some friends of mine own a house on Russian Hill where

cable cars clang past their picture window, and the street alongside them takes a precipitous drop straight to the bay, with a direct view of Alcatraz Island. Sequences in movies (mostly chase scenes) are shot on that street. And from their place it's an easy walk to Chinatown, with its pungent smells of spicy seafood, bustling shops, and visions of vibrant-colored signs in squiggles and slashes.

I'd love to look up my friends while I'm here, but I can't take time away from this case—too many lives may be endangered. I don't like these life-and-death matters anymore, having handled so many dicey situations in the FBI. Not that daily living isn't risky, but I think one's nerves can handle just so much stimulation in one lifetime.

Only because of David Bagley's involvement in this matter am I committed to seeing it through. Though I must admit I'm fascinated by the curves and sinkers someone's hurling at me. I don't need to hit a grand slam homer, but I hate standing in the box and whiffing every pitch.

I have a feeling that Damian Roberts, the kid who lives somewhere down there, might provide some tips I need on how to play this game. But I wonder if he's being evasive, what with his abrupt return to California from the funeral in Hillsboro. Besides, when I called him to set up an interview, all I got was his answering machine, so I sure hope he's not out of town.

We hit the tarmac with a solid, screeching thump, then glide forward against the restraint of loud, whining engines in reverse thrust mode. Once we've slowed, we taxi for what seems like ten minutes, then stop with a shudder and a wheeze. The fat man beside me, now awake to this grim life, gives his own loud groan as he stands, bends, and yanks his large briefcase from under the seat. He struggles into the aisle, reaches for the overhead bin and sets to tugging at another suitcase. Perspiration beads on his florid face.

There's a small space between his massive thigh and the seat, and I slide through it into the aisle. Glancing back, I notice a severe-looking man in a dark suit and a young lady in a red blazer who are trapped behind my traveling companion. Both have dark looks on their faces, obviously not wishing the oversize guy the best of health.

Once off the plane, I pull out my cell phone and try the Roberts kid again. I still get the machine, so I leave another short message, saying I need to talk with him and I'll call back once I find a hotel. Then I glance around, searching for a men's room.

Across the hall, at another bank of phones, I spot the disgruntled passenger in the dark suit. The lady in the blazer is nowhere in sight. The guy's staring at me as he holds a receiver to his ear, but he averts his eyes and turns away, talking with animation.

I make my pit stop, then head for the baggage carousel.

I'm in a better mood now, having found a comfortable motel room and eaten a tasty dinner of spaghetti and meatballs washed down with two icy beers. Another call to Roberts only nets me the same recorded message. I'm getting concerned.

I try Jeff Bagley at home in Hillsboro. He answers, and I run past him what I've learned. After I finish my spiel, there's a couple of seconds of silence.

"Damn, that's a tangled can of worms you've got there."

"Tell me about it. What did you find out from the Texas kid, Tanger?"

"I wish you'd been here. He was answering our questions, but not answering them, you know?"

"Like holding something back?"

"That's the feeling I had."

"Has he gone back to Texas?"

"Boots and all."

And so it goes in most investigations. Truth is a slippery commodity. Complete truth so ephemeral it might not exist on this planet.

I open my case binder and find the Avis rental list. Then I place a call to Marisol Vegas in D.C., my main woman in those long-ago days in balmy Puerto Rico when we tramped the tough streets and strolled the warm white beaches together. *Paradaiso.*

She answers and I politely say, "I've been having asthma lately, so to save me the heavy breathing, could you just say you'll have sex with me?"

There's a brief pause, a muffled giggle, then her bold, lilting voice that can charm a clam out of its shell says, "Sorry, honey, the Redskins' backfield is over here tonight. But there's a tight end on the team who might go for a no-balls *maricon* like you. Want his number?"

"I suppose so, since you've already got mine."

"Max, you're one of a kind. Easy to spot in a crowd."

"Even when they're gathered around you, you gorgeous spitfire."

"God, there you go with the stereotypical comments."

"Life's full of stereotypes, dear, that's what makes it so familiar."

"And such a pain in the ass, *verdad?*"

"You still didn't answer my question."

"Did I ever turn you down?"

"A time or two. I hope you haven't thrown me over for Ricky Martin."

"He's just *un joven,* a kid, *tu sabes.* I like mature macho men like you."

"Spoil me some more. I miss it."

"In a way, me too."

"But then there's your ever-escalating career in the Bureau."

She sighs. Unusual for her. "Yes, there's that. You'd never believe what a backbiting, suck-up place Headquarters can be."

"I've heard stories."

"They're all true. But sometimes you've got to go along to get along."

And I know that's not consistent with her fiercely independent nature. "Hang in there, *querida*. My money's still on you to become Director, then you can change everything."

"That's kind of you, *mi amor*. So, what's going on? Are you finally coming to visit me?"

Frightening images of Washington and its environs flash through my mind. I wipe perspiration from my brow. "You know I'd love to see you. Sorry I missed you on my trip to Florida."

"My fault, of course. I couldn't turn down the promotion, even if it did mean fighting the trench wars here at HQ."

"So, here's my latest mess." I give her a short rundown on the case I'm working.

"I'll give you this, Max, you get involved in some interesting stuff."

"Or screwed-up garbage. I know. Anyway . . ."

And I tell her about the rental vehicle that might've been used in the murder in Denver.

"So you're thinking because the guy who rented it is supposed to be from D.C.—"

"And you're there, queen of the computer section and all—"

"That I'll simply go input the data and the answers you

need will spit out, no problem."

"Isn't that how it works?"

"In the movies, and once in a great while even here at the Bureau."

"Could you check it out?"

"You know, *mi vida,* I wouldn't do it for anyone but you."

"So you *do* remember those steamy nights on the beach?"

"I remember getting tsetse fly bites on my butt while you fumbled around."

Not exactly how I recall it. Oh, well. "And you'll call me pronto?"

"I know everything is always rushed with you, *querido.*"

Well, I hope not everything.

Chapter 14

I slept fitfully last night, not used to the motel bed or city noises, and uneasy that I still wasn't able to reach Damian Roberts. This morning, after I shower and dress, I try once more, still only reaching his answering machine. Maybe he was out late last night and he's sleeping in.

I'm hungry, so I'll grab a sausage biscuit at a fast food spot. But then what? I juggle the rental car keys in my hand, then grab my suitcase. I'm not going to keep calling Roberts all day. I've got to find out where he is.

After two biscuits and a large OJ, my stomach comfortably greased, I consult the map I bought at the airport, finding Robert's location; it's a twenty-minute drive, unless I get lost or the traffic gets congealed like my food.

As I drive, I wonder if Marisol will get a hit on the name and the credit card number used to rent the Taurus in Denver. Could be my first real break in this case. Not that I believe in waiting for good fortune to solve a mystery, but it couldn't hurt.

Traffic's much heavier and more aggressive than in Hillsboro, but I try to go with the flow without plowing into anyone or getting run over. Somehow I manage, and I spot the apartment building I'm seeking. Finding a parking place comes a little harder, but patience finally pays off.

Here goes nothing, I think, though that's not usually a thought that flits through my head as I'm approaching an interview. Something about this case seems to be keeping me off balance. It's been bizarre, and I suppose I'm leery it will continue on that track. Sort of like a parallel universe where occurrences don't follow the physical rules you're used to. Pigs may fly and statues cry in such a weird world.

The building's older, but well-maintained, beige with white trim, four stories tall. Looks like maybe thirty or forty apartments. Roberts is on the third floor, so to work out my legs a bit, I hike up the stairs, wheezing as I reach the landing and search along the hallway for the right door.

I rap my knuckles, wait a bit, then knock again. The door swings open. I'm face-to-face with a gray-haired man with a lined ebony face accented by clouded brown eyes showing pain. "Yes?" he says.

"Is this the apartment of Damian Roberts?"

"It is." He examines me a moment. "Were you a friend of his?"

What? "I haven't met him, but I was hoping to talk with him about his company, Zipdata."

The tall, thin man stares at the floor a few seconds, then looks at me again with obvious effort. "Then you haven't heard?"

"I'm afraid not."

"You'd better come in."

We sit down in easy chairs a few feet apart. I'm assessing both him and the place for any vibes of danger. I don't really know who this is.

"Has something happened to Damian?" I sense I already know the answer.

A hefty, well-dressed woman walks in from the kitchen, seems startled when she sees me, but eases over to the man's side.

115

"This is Damian's mother," the man says. "I didn't catch your name."

"Max Austin. As I said, I came to talk with Damian."

She squints at me, then her head twists toward the man, her eyes beseeching him.

"I was just about to tell him what happened." He looks back at me and says, "Our boy was driving home late last night. He must've fallen asleep. Lost control of his car, then went off the road and struck a tree. He was . . . killed outright." He palms his face as if to stifle overwhelming emotion.

I'm stunned. I feel as if I'm in the middle of a special effects movie like *The Matrix*, or one of its successors, where you're never sure what's real and what's an illusion. "I'm very sorry," I say.

The man's head sags. The woman cries into a crumpled hanky, her hand on her husband's shoulder. In a while, he says, "What was it you needed from my son?"

"I'm a private investigator, working with the police on two murders of boys who were partners in Zipdata. I thought he might know something that would help me."

"Marvella, would you get us some coffee?" he says quietly.

She dabs her eyes, then slips out of the room.

"I knew the boy getting killed in Hillsboro was wrong," he says, "but I thought the Denver boy had a heart attack. And, as I said, Damian was killed in an accident. I don't understand what you're getting at."

"I'm not sure myself." I shrug. "Maybe I acquired too active an imagination working in the FBI. But it seems to me there must be some connection as to why these young men are dying."

"Why would Damian have known what it was?"

"I don't know if any of the partners know. But I need to find out."

"You think my son may have been killed on purpose?"

"I think it's a possibility."

"Oh, Lord." He rubs his face with both hands, then looks at me through watery eyes. "I was just hoping I could come to terms with losing my boy in an accident. You know, God's will and all. But I don't know if I can stand him being taken from us for some evil purpose."

Though it was awkward, the boy's parents allowed me to search his apartment. Everything looked normal to me for what a young computer nerd would have: various books on programming, stacked copies of *Wired* magazine, high-grade equipment, and lots of CDs. But one CD caught my eye, marked *Securegard.* They let me borrow it.

I would've run it on his computer except for the circumstances. Now as I'm flying back to Kansas City, I'm thinking I'll likely need help deciphering it. Maybe Pete Sanders will assist me. And it'd be nice to have Marisol Vegas there to make sure Pete's giving me the straight poop.

I tried calling Marisol before takeoff, but she was out. I hope she was gathering tons of information on the guy who came to Denver to kill a young computer genius. I'd like to give him some digits to compute. Some folded ones: my fist accessing his nose.

When I land in Kansas City, I call Pete Sanders. I get his answering machine and leave a message for him to call me on my cell phone. I won't get into Hillsboro until about four.

At the baggage carousel I pick up my suitcase, slide out the handle, then tilt it onto its wheels. My carry case is slung over my right shoulder. My leg's stiff from sitting on planes and gallivanting around airports, so I decide to stop for a pricey soft drink before the long drive home.

I spot a snack shop. Setting my bags down beside a table, I

head for the fountain. There are a couple of women in line ahead of me, so I stop, then glance back to make sure my luggage is okay.

And I spot him.

The same skinny guy I saw on my plane in Denver. At least, I think it's him. He scurries past the doorway.

And now I recall he might've been watching me make a phone call in the Denver airport. Did he have a flight to Kansas City, too? Or did he follow me here?

From Denver to San Francisco, then back to KCI. Odd itinerary. And he did look as though he were trying to avoid my glance.

I limp to the doorway and peer down the hallway. As I figured, he's like a meteor arcing through a black sky that you glimpse from the corner of your eye: by the time you turn your head to zero in, it's vanished. Damn.

I skip the drink and shuffle down the hallway, looking for the slim figure who seems to be tailing me. Maybe I'm just suffering jet lag, or early dementia. Getting old is not for sissies.

Back in Hillsboro, driving down the street to Sanders's house, I note his car's not there, so I study the area, pondering the case. The snow has started to melt. Some layers of white still coat the lawns, but the middle of the pavement is turning to slush.

Maybe I'll try to contact someone that we missed in our earlier neighborhood canvass. Sure enough, there's a Honda parked in the driveway of one house where no one was home before. An investigator's work is never done.

I park at the curb, two houses down from the house where the young musician pounds his ax night and day. A different type of string theory than that which rules the

Universe. At least, the adult Universe.

I ring the bell, and after a while an older woman peeks out at me with wary pale blue eyes, magnified greatly by her thick granny glasses. She's wearing a cotton house dress with yellow flowers on a sky blue background, topped off with a pink cardigan sweater. Old-fashioned diamond wedding ring set that's cutting into her finger.

"Yes?"

"My name's Max Austin, ma'am." I show her my ID. "Are you Mrs. Johnson?" Should be, that's the name on the wooden plaque beside the door.

"Why, yes. What is it?"

I tell her I'm working with the police on a case.

"Does this have to do with that poor boy who died?"

"Yes, it does. I'm looking for someone who—"

"I'm sorry, would you like to come in?"

I enter into a living room that's as musty and dated as a period setting in a museum. She indicates a battered sofa with a pattern that would be garish if it weren't so worn. I sink down, my haunch encountering the resistance of a spring that aspires to poke through the upholstery.

She settles into a rocking chair and revs herself into a rhythmic cadence. "You were saying?"

"Are you usually here during the day, Mrs. Johnson?"

"Except when I go grocery shopping or to play bridge on Thursday afternoons. I don't get out much in the cold weather. Particularly when it's snowy, like lately."

"Then I'm wondering if you saw anyone or anything unusual in the neighborhood the past few days."

She raises her chin, staring at the ceiling, thinking. Rocking. Maybe she's fallen asleep.

She finally says, "You mean someone suspicious?"

I nod. "Like that."

"No, I can't think of anyone. Except maybe some of those long-hair freaks that visit the hippie that lives a couple of houses down that way."

I believe she means our musician friend. "I was thinking more of someone in a delivery van or truck that didn't seem to belong in this neighborhood."

She shrugs and stares back at the ceiling.

I sigh. "Then thank you for—"

"Well, there were those two men in a white van a few days ago."

"Two men?"

"They parked next door in front of Madge Bleaker's house. She's always off somewhere shopping or getting her hair done. Don't know who she thinks she's going to impress."

And I remember the narcissistic Mrs. Bleaker didn't recall seeing a van.

"I thought maybe they had a delivery for her. Sometimes they come here when she's gone and ask me to hold a package for her. As if I got nothing better to do. But they never even went to her door. They just looked across the street for a few minutes, then they left."

"Did you get a good look at them?"

"They was just middle-aged men. One of them was kinda skinny." Then she snorts, laughing to herself about something.

"What?" I ask.

"I was just thinking they'd probably like to have some of that extra hair those kids have hanging down in their faces."

"How's that?"

"The driver was bald as an eagle, and the skinny guy had a rug."

"A toupee?"

"Yep, not a good one, neither."

"How did you happen to notice that?"

"I saw him reach up under one edge and scratch his head. Sorta made me laugh. I'm not sure Madge don't have one herself. It's hard to tell, it's sprayed up so stiff all the time, you know?"

"I see what you mean."

And I leave, thinking about the two men, wondering if the skinny one could possibly be my slinky shadow. As I start to cross the street, a brown cocker spaniel darts past me without regard to whatever cars, trucks, or motorcycles may be forging down the pavement. He slips in the snow packed against the curb, and I quickly check the street for vehicles. None are coming, except for a street cleaner making a loud, grinding noise, which lumbers toward my SUV. Guess I'd better move it.

I step over the dog's track, thinking that, with the big, revolving brush headed this way, the doggie's imprint will soon be erased, much as all our traces across this planet will disappear with time and erosion . . .

Wait a minute.

Chapter 15

I hustle to the front of my SUV, take a glance at the snowy remains stretching away from the curb, then trot back toward the street cleaner, waving my arms for him to stop. The driver slows, then grudgingly halts the machine, though its huge brush still revolves in a menacing way. He sticks his head out the window to address me; he's not smiling.

"Hey, pal," he yells, "move that damn truck."

Approaching him, I flash my ID.

"Police business," I say. "I need you to skip this side of the street for a minute."

He scratches his scraggly beard, lifts and resettles a grungy ball cap on a thicket of unruly hair, then spits out something brown, missing my shoes by inches.

"My brother-in-law's a cop," he pronounces. "That ain't no city badge. You're some kinda P.I., or whatever."

"Absolutely right, buddy, but I'm working with the police on a case. We could call and confirm it with them, but that'd take longer than it would for me to snap a couple of pictures, then I'll move out of your way."

He blows out an exasperated breath. "Why don't you take the pictures after I clean? It'll look real nice then."

"Come here," I say, motioning to him.

He stares at me.

I limp to the back of my SUV, extract my 35mm Minolta, and keep waving for him to follow.

He kills the motor, then clambers down out of the elevated cab. Big son of a gun. Hands the size of baseball gloves. "I don't know what the fuck you think—"

"Look there," I say, pointing at some flattened snow beside the curb.

"What?"

"See the impression—those squiggles?"

"Like tire tracks?"

"You got it." I snap a couple of pictures.

He rubs his chin whiskers. "What kinda case you workin'?"

"Murder."

"No shit?"

"Really. Can I borrow your cap?"

"Uh, I guess so." He hands it over.

I lay it beside the tire track. "Shows relative size," I tell him.

Looks like the van pulled out at a sharp angle, leaving a good front tire print without running over it with the back tire. The back tire impressions are too overlaid to be of any value. I snap several more shots.

"Some kinda truck tire, huh?" he says.

"Or delivery van."

"Mmm hmm. Could be that, too. That what you're looking for?"

"Exactly."

"You're lucky I didn't rub it out."

"Very. I was going to offer you twenty bucks to leave it alone. Still will, for that matter." I hand him back his cap.

He smiles, showing beige teeth. "You got a business card, forget the twenty. I can tell my brother-in-law I helped work a murder case. All he does is hand out speeding tickets."

And so, cooperation by the citizenry in fighting crime once

more pays off. I'm pretty sure the FBI lab will be able to tell me the make of tire from this tread imprint. And that'll put me in the hunt again.

I stop at the Zercher Photo Shop on Wanamaker where they do one-hour developing. I pace around looking harried, so they either take pity or decide to avoid more aggravation, and the clerk hands me my finished pics in under twenty minutes. On the way home, I stop to pick up Binga at the kennel.

Stopping by the mailbox out front, I find it half full, mostly with bills and sales pamphlets. As I wheel into my gravel drive, the Sun slides below the treetops on the western border of my yard like a worn, bloody warrior retreating to mend his wounds. My truck rolls to a halt, and Binga piles out.

Seemingly elated to be home, Binga cavorts about the yard for at least a minute as I sort through the mail. Then she seems to realize she's no longer a pup and resignedly plops her tired haunches to the ground, her tongue lolling, panting hard. I retrieve her food bowl from the porch, and she leans forward and licks my hand in a gesture of gratitude.

Inside, I pause by the phone. Two messages, the first from Marisol: "Call me when you get in. I couldn't reach you on your cell phone."

I turned off my phone during the drive from the airport to Hillsboro so I could think. Then I forgot about it. Gee, out of touch with the hectic world for a couple of hours; how wonderful.

The second is from Amy, checking to see if I'm home yet. So I call her at work and we catch up on what's been going on with her, then I tell her I've developed some clues in the case, not going into detail. Mostly, we've both been working our butts off and wish we had a little more leisure time. I think, but don't say, that we could spend some of it together.

Then I get up my nerve.

"Would you like to have lunch tomorrow?"

"You mean together?"

I've obviously caught her off guard. "That was the idea."

"You know, I think that would be nice."

She seems to be warming to the notion.

We discuss the possibilities, deciding we'll try some Indian cuisine at The Globe. After I hang up, I spend a few moments imagining the scenario. Then, as I glance outside at the Sun gleaming on the remnants of snow in my yard, I find myself thinking about Karen Bartles, the fair lieutenant in Denver. She certainly has charms that stoke my libidinous impulses. Ah, well. I must admit, my love connections are a bit tangled at the moment.

Anyway, I still have business to conduct. But before I can make that call to Marisol, Binga begins to whine, giving me her "starving pet" look. So I change gears and fill her bowl. That done, I grab a beer and the phone and collapse in my easy chair to dial the great state of Virginia.

I get Marisol on the first try. She sounds tense.

"*Corazon*, it's me," I say. "Sorry I killed my cell phone earlier."

"*Esta bien, mi amor.* But I'm glad you called. Do you remember our friend, the Duke, in *La Perla?*"

She's talking about a drug lord we worked a case on in a crime-ridden area in San Juan, Puerto Rico. Why she's brought that up, I don't know. "Sure, what about him?"

"He called me at work this afternoon. Said he got the titles on those three pieces of property you and I were interested in on the island. Since there might be some problems to iron out, I thought we should get together ASAP and discuss our options."

"Is it something we could talk about now?" What she's saying makes no sense at all, so I'm trying to figure out if she's giving me some kind of coded message.

"No, there are too many variables. Other people are interested in the properties, too. We need to move fast."

Okay, now I think I get it. She mentioned "titles" and "three pieces of property." Title III is the section of the United States Code which allows federal agencies to use wiretaps. The FBI had one on Duke in Puerto Rico, listening in on his drug deals, gathering evidence against him.

So I think she's saying she believes her phone, or mine, may be tapped. Therefore, she wants to talk in person. Right away.

"I'm available anytime. Where do you want to meet?" Maybe she came up with something on the guy I asked her to run through the databases.

"I've never been to the Heartland before, which you describe so glowingly, so maybe I'll call your bluff. Meet me at that restaurant you said you'd take me to someday. Six o'clock tomorrow night."

"You got it. Can I ask you a favor?"

"*Seguro.*"

"I'm going to fax you some artwork. Could you check with your expert buddy there to see if he can authenticate the artist who painted it?"

A moment's pause. "Of course." And she gives me her fax number.

After we hang up, I send her copies of the tire treads I photographed in the snow across the street from where Mossler was killed.

That done, I fix myself a PB&J sandwich and a glass of milk and sit down at my dining room table to chew and think. Mostly, I'm wondering what Marisol found out that's so important she'd drop her work and fly to Kansas to tell me. Maybe the guy is someone they've got a case on and she's trying to wave me off until they finish their investigation.

But why not just tell me so? Why all the coded conversations and the paranoia about tapped phones? It's all so out of character for Marisol.

What have I gotten into this time?

The phone rings, and I startle. Must be Marisol again. Or Amy.

"I just wanted to let you know," says Lieutenant Bartles in her sultry, cultured voice, "how sorry I was that I missed seeing you before you left Denver."

"Karen! Is that really you?" Can I be suave, or what? "You know, I felt bad about that, too. I'm glad you called, it's good to hear your voice."

A pause. "And thanks for not asking what's going on in our case, so I'd have to think of some bullshit to use as an excuse."

"I was hoping your call might not be business."

"To be candid, Max, it's not that often I run across someone I enjoy talking with as much as I did with you. I was hoping we could keep in touch."

"I'd like that, Karen. You know, the flight between here and there is pretty short."

"Maybe you could wing it out this way again soon."

"Or you could come here. There are some good museums and places to eat in Kansas City. I'd enjoy showing you around."

"I was interested in seeing your place in the country, too. It sounds very relaxing. I loved visiting my grandparents' farm when I was growing up."

"I'll bet we could work that out."

"That'd be nice. Anyway, I've been as brazen as I can

muster for one night, so I'd better let you go."

"I'm still busy with this case, but I'll give you a call in a couple of weeks and we'll make definite plans."

"Sounds great. Are you making some progress?"

"Frankly, I don't know." It strikes me that when people used to tell me something "frankly," I knew they were lying. "There are some weird things that've come up, Karen. They might be something, or maybe nothing."

"Such as?"

The ever curious cop. Maybe that's why I never dated one. You both view each other too suspiciously.

For some reason, I hesitate to tell her. Am I worried about a phone tap? I hope it's not because I doubt her. "I found a witness who saw the tag number on that white van that was seen before the murder here."

"Have you tracked it down?"

"No, it's only a partial plate, so there are over a hundred possibles."

"But you'll get the answer eventually."

"Hopefully. Crime operates in a mysterious universe, and sometimes the secret to a scheme can only be unlocked with a special key. Sort of the way we think black holes may be the key to the creation and destruction of star systems."

"So you really do think like an astronomer."

"Hardly. But it seems the mechanics of the Universe operate even on the microscopic scale of earthly enterprises."

"I'll have to take your word for it. I almost flunked Physics 101 in college."

Come to think of it, so did I.

Chapter 16

The way Marisol was acting bothers me. She's not a paranoid person. Usually.

But just to be safe, I open the downstairs closet, rummage in my handy dandy private eye kit, and extract a gizmo I bought in Kansas City that's used to detect taps on telephones. I attach it to my phone line, check the readings, and conclude that my line seems clear. I also look over my telephone's handset, seeing nothing unusual.

After I stash the kit back in the closet and settle into my leather chair to ponder the situation, the strangeness of Marisol's call whirls in orbit with other peculiar episodes in this case: the odd behavior of the cops, both in Hillsboro and Denver, the phone warning I received, and the possibility I was being followed. Not to mention the bizarre murders themselves. Then add in the puzzling nature of Zipdata's contracts with both private companies and government agencies, possibly involving breached national security through the use of a Trojan horse.

I glance at my sports coat hanging on the back of a chair in the dining room. Extracting the CD I got in Denver from the side pocket, I head upstairs. Might as well see if I understand any of it.

I flip on the light in my small office, then freeze. My computer's on, with something typed on the screen. Definitely not the way I left it before my trip to Denver.

I start toward it, then stop, sucking in a breath as I realize someone might want me to do just that. So I ease back out of the room. Binga's apparently still conked out on her mat downstairs, obviously not as sharp of hearing and sniffing as she once was. In her younger days, if someone had broken in the place, she'd have taken their leg off. I tiptoe down the hall to my bedroom, where I pause and listen for any sounds.

Nothing; I snap on the light. Everything seems in order, so I step over to the bookcase where I keep a revolver in a vase of dried flowers. The hard steel feels comforting in my sweaty hand.

I peek in the closet and under the bed. Zip. Looking in the bathroom, I find it empty, as well. So I slip back into the office. Only place to hide in here is behind two large filing cabinets against the wall; I get an angle, then stick my head and gun around the sturdy equipment. No one back there.

I'm pretty sure the house is empty, but I suppose I'd better check it out. And so I proceed, room by room, listening hard to the tiniest sounds, flicking on the lights, entering with my eyes wide open, my gun sweeping the area before me. I find nothing but the stale air of unused space.

Now all that's left to inspect is the basement. An unfinished and creepy basement. During tornado conditions, I'm glad to head down there for the structural safety afforded, but in this case, I'm far from thrilled about descending into the clutter and dankness of the little-used, neglected room. Especially since it might be harboring a criminal. As I creep down the stairway, one measured step at a time, the unpainted wooden planks creak under my weight, and a damp blanket of basement air gives me a chill.

Jumbled stacks of empty cardboard boxes, a clattering forced-air furnace, and a sixty-gallon hot water heater all provide fine spots of concealment for a bad guy to lie in wait. The two overhead light bulbs set at opposite ends of the cement room cast a pale light, making me strain my eyes to carry out my mission to search and destroy. Twelve-inch air ducts wrapped with silvery-gray insulation and a web of shiny copper water pipes run amok across the unfinished ceiling. I shine my flashlight from place to place, gun barrel following the small, bright circle, hoping to pin the guy down, to make him surrender.

There's a stack of boxes to my left, and I give it a shove, listening to the sharp clatter as stiff cardboard edges smack the concrete floor. No one leaps out at me, so I wipe the sweat from my brow, then continue searching, trying to find the guy, but hoping not to. I'd rather steer clear of a direct confrontation.

After a couple of minutes, I've cleared the room—no one there. Blowing out a sigh of relief, I climb the stairs back to the first floor to begin a new search, trying to find where the guy got in. As I survey the bathroom, I spot a broken window and creep over to find the screen's been cut. There are damp splotches on the carpet. Someone climbed in with snow on their shoes.

I head outside. Shining my flashlight on the ground beneath the busted-out window, I spot a mushy place, but with no good footprints visible. And no burglar tools have been left behind.

I go back in the house, miffed. Back in my study, I read the message on the screen: IT IS A GOOD THING TO LEARN CAUTION FROM THE MISFORTUNES OF OTHERS. PUBLILIUS SYRUS.

Okay, I think that's a threat. But, of course, not one direct enough to charge anyone with. That is, if I had the slightest idea who to point a finger at.

My computer components seem to be intact. The CD

holder has been moved, but as I flip through the CDs, I don't find any missing. There's nothing anyone would have wanted, anyway.

I consider calling the sheriff's department, but decide it's not worth the time spent waiting for them to arrive. Then I'd have to answer useless questions so they could fill out a form to file. So, instead, I insert the Securegard CD and bring it up.

Napoleon said the sword will always be conquered by the spirit. And my spirit is getting fired up. Let the games begin.

Morning comes too soon, and I yawn and stretch, then roll out of bed to start another day. Unfortunately, as I feared, I couldn't glean much from the Securegard CD. I'll need Pete Sanders and maybe Will Tanger to help me understand what it's about. And no more bullshit about company secrets. This is life and death we're talking about. I need to know all.

Marisol calls before I finish loading the dishes into the machine. "My friend checked out your painting," she says. Ah, she means the tire tread marks.

"Any luck?"

"He knew the artist. I'm sending verification on your machine."

"You guys do good work."

"We try."

I give her my fax number, shuffle downstairs to let Binga outside, then hustle back up to my office, where the machine is already whirring into action.

The tire tread's on a Trail Buster Radial APR, size LT 235/75 R15. All right, something concrete to work with. But now I have to find them.

First, I'll check the rental agencies in Hillsboro. That failing, I'll try Kansas City. It seems those would be the two best bets for finding the van used by the guys who killed Kyle Mossler.

But first, I call Pete Sanders. He sounds distracted, depressed. I soon learn why.

"My grandma took a bad fall yesterday, broke her hip in two places. My mom and I were at the hospital all night. They're going to operate in a few hours, and I'm getting cleaned up and grabbing some clothes and stuff before I go back to the hospital."

"I'm real sorry to hear that. I do need your help with some computer stuff, but it can wait." I don't think he'll be too sharp at this point, anyway.

"If she makes it through the operation all right, I'll feel a lot better. I'll call you when I get home."

"I'll be out most of the day," I say, then give him the number of my overworked cell.

I spend the morning visiting vehicle rental agencies around Hillsboro. Some of them don't have vans for rent. Of those that do, a couple don't have white or light beige ones. I find a few possibilities, but when I look over the type of tire and the tread design, I find no match for the mysterious van.

I arrive at the restaurant for my lunch date with Amy. She looks even more gorgeous than usual, like a diamond kissed by sunlight. And despite some awkward moments in the beginning, we soon fall into a relaxed and friendly conversation. Altogether, I have a great time, and I'm sorry that I have to cut it short to handle some more business.

So it's on to Kansas City. I'll still have several hours to work before I meet Marisol at the Plaza III steakhouse. On the drive there, I let the facts of the case float through my mind, occasionally colliding like asteroids hitting planets, hoping the explosive force will jar loose a new idea in my brain.

Past Le Compton, Lawrence, and Leavenworth. Through the toll booth, paying, getting the computerized receipt. Hard to believe society functioned before computers became widely available.

Of course, much like cars, planes, or television sets, the modern devices have brought with them a whole new set of problems. What price convenience? With all the viruses, stolen identities, and tracking of our purchases, rentals, and interests, computers constantly invade our privacy and right to solitude. Big Brother is watching, listening, intercepting. Corporate or governmental, or both.

Marisol seemed concerned about a wiretap on one of our phones. There wasn't one on mine, but still, if that guy was following me, he seemed to have a pretty good idea where I was going. Maybe even what I intended to do when I got there.

I take the 435 exit north, toward the Kansas City airport, recalling my recent trips to Denver and San Francisco.

Denver, where the cops suddenly got sloppy and uncooperative. Where I might've been followed by some guy who happened to fit witnesses' descriptions of a guy in a van in Hillsboro and at the park in Denver. A skinny fellow. Dark suit. Toupee? I was too far away to notice. And I saw no bald man taking any interest in me.

Then on to San Francisco, where my interview never happened.

Oh, my God. Could my trip to San Francisco have caused the car "accident" that killed Damian Roberts? Should I have heeded the warnings and not gotten involved in this? Maybe I'm to blame for all the deaths beyond the first one. Maybe it's endangering David Bagley and even Jeff, as well as Pete Sanders and the Tanger kid, for me to be investigating this case.

Or maybe they're all marked already, by some person or group that wants to wipe out their company. My gut reaction is that only by finding out what's going on can I help anyone. But who on Earth would want to murder a bunch of computer nerds?

I sense that it has to be connected with the Securegard program. With the Trojan horse inserted in it. Planted by Kyle Mossler and Will Tanger.

I swing off at the 152 exit. I'll arrive at the airport in ten minutes. Hopefully, to find the rental van and get some useful clues.

Did I mention to anyone that I was going to contact these rental agencies? I don't think so. I check my rearview mirror; no one seems to be following me. Still, it seems as if someone has been prescient at predicting every move I've been making. Have the cops been giving away my plans to someone? To the murderer?

That makes little sense, especially since a cop's kid is at risk in Hillsboro, and, besides, there are two agencies in two different states involved. But the cops in both departments seem to have withdrawn their help soon after I contacted them and told them what I intended to do. That seems crazy.

After all, who else would be interested in these murders? And how would they keep up with what I'm doing? I'm still drawing a blank as I pull into a parking lot at the terminal.

I grab my binder and shove open the door, ready to check out the car rental agencies. Then I freeze, one leg dangling out of my vehicle, my mouth hanging open as a sudden realization hits me. Son of a bitch.

Chapter 17

I lay my hand atop my case binder. It's the fancy one the Hillsboro detectives gave me, telling me it was the chief's idea for me to have it. But when I thanked him, he seemed unaware of it. So where did it come from? And, more importantly, where has it been?

It's been with me, for most of the time I've been investigating this case. But who had it before me? I have an idea, or at least a conjecture. Then again, maybe I've watched too many mystery shows on the tube. Or read too many novels about crafty detectives.

It couldn't hurt to take a peek, if only to lay my wild suspicions to rest. So I remove the pages and lay them on the seat next to me. Then I examine the binder itself. It's a bit thick, as though it were padded or something.

Or something.

Why would it be thicker than the normal binder? I pull my small, sharp knife from my pocket. Probe one end of the binder. It seems tight. But . . .

I flip it open, then draw the blade along the length of the inside of the end cover. This slits it all the way open. It looks like there's something inside there.

I make another long slash, horizontally from the top end of the first cut, then peel the flap open. Yes, there's definitely something embedded inside the cover. And it looks like what I suspected.

A microphone. With a transmitter. In a flat configuration such as I've never seen before. Very sophisticated. Probably expensive.

Who in the hell would have access to something like this? And why would they be using it on me? Not the police, I'm pretty sure; at least, I've never seen them use such a device.

So I'm guessing if someone gave it to them, then the "someone" monitored what I was doing. At the least, they learned what I developed in my investigation. At worst, they may have killed witnesses before I could contact them.

And I think this implies they controlled the Denver detectives as well as those from Hillsboro. But who would have that much clout? Plus the wherewithal to make such a sophisticated device. And the authority to use it. Damn.

"Man, I can't believe this parking lot is so friggin' full," I say. The mechanism advances a bit, then stops. Voice-activated, naturally. I scan the parking lot for guys in a car somewhere nearby, monitoring the transmission. I don't see anyone. But maybe the transmitter's more powerful than I think. And it could be they can retrieve the information by rewinding the recorder electronically, then monitoring the replay.

Whatever. I start to say something satisfying like "kiss my glutes," when I have a better idea. For the time being, I leave the binder in my car, slam the door, and head for the terminal. In spite of this setback, I need to keep working the case, so I'll cover some more leads on the phantom van.

I want to play this correctly. Make the right moves. Insure the validity of the old adage: Payback's a bitch.

My contacts with employees at the car rental companies are going well. So far only one outfit refused to show me their records because the airport's in Missouri and I have a Kansas

P.I. license. And I did wheedle the girl into checking to see if they had any white vans for rent, which they didn't, so I was still able to mark them off my list.

Problem being, there are only three rental companies to go. I don't want to come up empty. Fingers crossed.

I approach the guy at the Dollar counter. He's gray at the temples, like me, more wrinkled than I, and looks weary. Handling car rentals is probably not the most rewarding job in the world.

"May I help you, sir?"

At least he seems friendly.

I give him my spiel about an important investigation, flashing my ID quickly, and leading into my question about what vans they have for rent.

He gives me a corner of the mouth smile. "I'm a retired Kansas City cop," he says. "You're a little out of your jurisdiction."

"I was FBI for twenty-five," I say. "I'm helping out the Hillsboro PD. Need to get this covered as soon as possible."

"Can't do it," he says.

"Heck," I say, still looking at him in my most professional manner.

He grabs a book and thumbs through it. "Officially, that is."

"Any information is a help right now."

He stops at a page. "I just had a phone call about vans and was going to take a look at our list. Yep, I think the caller might like either this white Chevy van or the white Ford Econoline we have out on the lot."

"They sound like nice vehicles."

"I was going to step outside and make sure they're ready to go. Would you like to come along, get some fresh air?"

"I love fresh air."

He motions to a young girl reading a magazine in the back, then says for her to take over the counter while we're gone.

"Name's George. I worked on that case where one of your agents got murdered," he says as we stride toward the waiting fleet of vehicles.

I recall the matter, as I also worked the case. The agent was visiting from D.C. and ended up in the wrong place, putting himself at the bad end of a robbery. Then he pulled his gun, the robber jumped him, and the whole thing turned to crap. The shooter was later caught. Too late to benefit the agent, though.

"We appreciated your help," I say.

"No problem. Ah, here's the Ford."

I look it over. It fits the general description. And I examine the front tires. Nope, they're Goodyears. Not a match to our tire tread print, unless maybe they've just been rotated. I look at the back tires, too. Still nothing.

On to the Chevy. It's plain and white, you could put a magnetic sign on the side and it'd look like a business van. The left front tire is a Trail Buster. Ditto the right front one. And the rear ones. Bingo.

"This one look good?"

"Just great, George."

"Hmmm. There's a little ding in the edge of the door there. Maybe I'll look at our records to see who was driving it about . . ."

"Looks about a week old to me," I say.

"That's what I thought, too. So, that's what I'll check."

Ah, the camaraderie of law enforcement.

I get the name, address, and credit card number used to rent the van. The name's different from the one used in Denver, but the address is in Virginia. I think maybe . . . ah, I'm back at my truck with the intrusive case binder, so I can leaf through my records. Yep, the credit card is the same type as that one used out west. Different number, though.

Little less than two hours until I meet Marisol at the Plaza III steakhouse. Gives me time to do some diversion driving and check for a tail, plus think this matter over. Also to plan the logistics of our get-together.

A horse stops at the intersection, decked out in fancy traces leading back to a shiny black carriage, and I walk past him, close enough to smell the acrid-leathery scent of the big bay's sweat. I've been ambling around the Plaza, a section of Kansas City devoted to classy restaurants, high-end retail shopping, specialty shops, bookstores, and boutiques. It's crowded with bustling tourists, fashionably dressed young couples strolling about as much to be seen as to see, and the younger set with their in-your-face hairstyles, body piercings, and tight, brief clothes in various dusky colors.

Cigarettes are the accessory of choice. Everyone seems desperate to be noticed, but none wants to be caught noticing others. But I'm here to study the setup, not the people, though the two may intertwine here, as do double star systems.

I examine the various routes to and from the restaurant. Then I study the foot traffic and the flow of the cars. Also the timing patterns of the horse-drawn carriages meandering along the busy streets.

Now I enter the restaurant. It's quiet. Not yet time for crowds to press inside and heighten the decibels with their loud, incessant chatter.

"May I help you, sir?" says a young man with improbably blond hair in a spiky do.

"I'm with *The Kansas City Star*," I lie, nonchalantly.

"That's cool," he says, but I sense he's not impressed.

"I told the owner I'd be writing an article about your restaurant, but I didn't know exactly when I'd come by. Turns out that now's a good time for me. Could I look around a little?" I start moving, which gets him in motion, too.

"I guess so, but we got customers coming in pretty soon. Is this gonna take long?"

"Just a few minutes for the basic inspection. Then I'll let you go. I'm meeting someone later for my meal."

"What d'ya want to see?"

"Kitchen, bathrooms, exits. Just the physical layout." I push my way into the kitchen, glance around at the busy chefs commanding various stainless steel countertops, their hands swift and skillful.

Then I see what I'm searching for. I head for the back door, stopping to admire a filled pastry cart. It looks scrumptious. "Nice variety," I comment.

Blond head nodding. He's looking at everything but me. Good.

I march over to the back door. It's alarmed. "Can you flip this off?" I ask. "I just want to peek outside."

"Sure, I guess so." He does. I make a mental note.

The door swings open, and I step outside, looking both ways, checking the possibilities. Satisfied, I step back inside. "Make sure you keep the area around the door completely clear. No boxes stacked out here, anything like that. Could get people killed."

"Oh, sure. Right. No problem." He brushes back his hair. Not a bad-looking kid.

We make our way back through the kitchen. "I'll just check the restroom, then I'll wait outside for my date," I say, smiling. "You can go on with what you were doing, I'll be okay. I know you're busy."

"Yeah, okay."

141

Having observed his nametag, I say, "And, Chris, I'm going to mention to your boss how helpful you were."

He brightens a bit. "Cool."

I duck into the men's room, which is small, two urinals and one stall, couple of sinks, no rear exit. Fine. No problems I foresee here.

Back out front, I lean against the building and watch the street. No one seems to pay me any mind, and I see no one I recognize. No bald guys eyeballing me. No skinny guys with rugs lurking in doorways. Cosmic.

Within ten minutes, Marisol appears at the corner, glances behind her, then turns toward me. She looks even better than the beautiful girl I remember; she's now a poised and exquisite woman. Too bad this is business, I could get excited about having a par-tay.

"Hey, gorgeous," I say.

"Max! I don't think anyone followed me. At least, if they tried, I'm pretty sure I shook them."

"Nice to see you, too."

She smiles. Tight, nerves taut at the corners. But nice.

"Come here," she says, arms outstretched, then gives me a strong hug, her breasts pushing hard against my thumping heart. "I missed you, you big *cabron*."

Not a compliment, but I think she's kidding. I hug her back, trying to catch my breath. This is fine. "Good to see you, *querida*," I say.

Her eyes light up like glowing marbles, then she blinks rapidly. "We've got big trouble. Let's go inside."

Chapter 18

The smile drops off my face, and I open the door to the restaurant.

The cooperative blond waiter is nowhere in sight. We're approached by a striking black-haired young lady. I request a booth in an area not far from the kitchen, flashing a ten, and she gives me a radiant smile and seats us at almost the perfect spot.

"You've gotten more generous since I knew you," Marisol says.

"It's business," I tell her. "I can still tell a bill's denomination by squeezing it in my pocket. No use being a spendthrift, I always say."

"With you, I doubt there's any danger of that."

We sit. We both check around for anything threatening. Then our eyes meet across the table.

"You say we have problems?" I ask.

She reaches across the table to take my hand. My heart has barely slowed since that first warm hug, and now it kicks up another few notches. In a low voice, she says, "When I ran the guy who rented the car in Denver, I got *nada*. No arrests, no credit record, no military service. Zero."

"What are you saying?"

"The American Express card was good. The account exists. Which means the man who has it should, too. But I couldn't bring up anything. That's not consistent with a

143

person with a credit card who travels and rents vehicles."

"I'm not sure what you're—"

"I think it's a phony name. Possibly a totally phony—"

"Hello, my name's Jonathan," says a beefy young waiter with short hair and a counterfeit smile. "Can I get you something to drink?"

I glance at Marisol. She shrugs. "Bring me a frozen margarita. A big one."

My eyebrows go up. "Coors Lite in a bottle," I say.

Marisol regards our waiter as he walks away. I glance around the room once more. No one seems to be observing us.

"Max, I think it could be a cover. The card must belong to some corporate or government entity, and my guess would be the latter. But they're not admitting it's theirs."

I take a deep breath. This doesn't compute. "You're saying the guy's some type of government agent? And the agency's trying to hide it?"

She drums bright red fingernails on the tabletop, then exhales through her nose. "I know it sounds far-fetched."

"Because the car was used in a murder?"

"That, and because I can't imagine why an agency would be so secretive about an agent's travel. Unless he was doing some undercover work. But even if he were, why would he just happen to show up at the park where that kid got killed?"

She's got me there. "Oh," I say, remembering.

"What?"

I take out my notepad and leaf through it. "Here we go," I say, pointing at a page. "I just got this at the airport. A different guy rented the van that was probably used in the Hillsboro murder, but he did use an American Express card, just like the guy in Denver."

She takes the notepad, at the same time pulling a small cell phone from her purse.

"Here we go, folks," says the waiter, setting down a huge margarita with a salted rim. Then he gives me a beer bottle beaded with sweat and a frosted mug. Now, that's the ticket.

We thank him, each take a gulp, and Marisol returns her attention to punching in numbers on her phone.

"What are you doing?" Curious as a cat.

"Internet access," she says. "I'll get my server, then e-mail John, give him the info, and he'll run it for us."

"Amazing." I do well to punch in the right numbers to make a phone call.

She enters the commands, then folds up the phone and drops it back in her purse.

Hoisting her margarita again, she gives me a weary smile. "*Salud.*"

"And to your health, success, and prosperity," I retort, then take a slug.

"I'd settle for getting this little enigma straightened out," she says.

"That's a start," I agree.

Then her eyes suddenly open wide.

"What?" I ask.

"*Hijo de puta,*" she says, which isn't very ladylike, but I can tell something has startled her. "Don't look. Behind you about three booths over is a guy I know."

"So?"

"The credit card used to rent the car in Denver, Max. I knew the name on it had a familiar ring—Phil Martinson—but I couldn't place it."

"And now you can?"

"*Si,* it's him—that man. I met him at a summit meeting in D.C. a few months ago. It didn't register with me because everyone just called him Bones."

I'm dying to twist around. "Summit meeting?"

"*Tu sabes,* one of those get-togethers where lots of agencies with a similar problem meet to brainstorm, maybe get some ideas going, form little groups to address certain areas."

"What problem was that?"

"Computer security for agencies' files. Everyone in government has problems with illicit crackers. And it's getting worse, not better. So the White House sent a mandate to come up with some workable solutions."

"Who was there?"

"CIA, FBI, NSA, Secret Service, U.S. Marshals. Any agency with secrets to safeguard and investigative experience in tracking infiltrators and keeping them out, maybe catching them as they try to enter the systems."

"And the guy was there?"

"I'm sure it's him. I remember he stared at me all through the meeting, never mind the ring on his finger. Gave me those . . . what it is? Those creeps."

"Tell me more about the meeting."

"That was for insiders only. Government agencies."

"What agency was he with?"

"*No se.* I can't remember."

"What's he look like?"

"Middle-aged, skinny, severe-looking face. Pale, sort of a career bureaucrat look to him."

Hijo de puta zips through my head. "Is he wearing a cheap dark suit?"

"Yes, how do you—"

"Maybe a rug?"

She glances randomly around the room, then zeroes in over my shoulder. "Can't tell for sure, but it might be."

"He alone?"

"He's with a stocky bald guy who has his back to us."

Of course. For a moment I consider lurching out of the booth and stomping over there. Getting in their faces. Trying to pin down who they are and why they're following me. Us.

But then, the investigation I've done suggests they may be murderers. And it could be they think I'm onto them. Which means they're a definite threat to me.

Threats. Two since I started working this case.

"Where'd you go, Max?"

She's staring at me oddly.

"Sorry, I was just thinking."

Worse yet, I realize, they're a threat to Marisol. And with two of them here and with the need to protect her, a confrontation wouldn't be very smart. I need to find out more about who they are and what they're after before I know how to handle them.

"I'm going to the john," I say.

"You haven't even finished one beer."

"It's business, not pleasure. If one of them follows me, you watch for your chance, then hustle into the kitchen. Wait for me by the back door."

"If he doesn't?"

"Sit tight, I'll think of something else." At least, I hope I will.

I take another comforting swig of my alcoholic Rocky Mountain water, then shove out of my seat and skirt the booths at the other end of the room, peeking toward the far booth as I round the corner. Oh, yeah. I think it's the same dour-looking, lanky fellow who followed me before.

I push open the door to the restroom, grab a handful of paper towels, dump them into one urinal, then wait at the door, holding it open just a crack. Sure enough, in about thirty seconds, I spot a husky bald guy headed this way. I step over and establish myself at the good urinal, then reach over and flush the plugged one.

The guy enters and nonchalantly surveys the situation; he's a big sucker. Now water begins to overflow the bowl. He hesitates, winces, then pushes his way into an empty stall. The door bangs shut behind him, and I bolt for the door, being careful not to slip in the pooling liquid that's sluicing across the floor.

I grab the arm of a passing waiter. "Hey," I say, "you're not going to believe this, but there's some guy in the head who's stopping up the urinal. Water's running all over the place."

He stares at me, his mouth open. I clutch his shoulder and give him a little push in the direction of the door. "You'd better check it out before he does a lot of damage."

Uncertainly, he advances toward the john. I limp over to the corner and take a quick peek, spotting the skinny guy who looks like a hawk with a pinched face. Yep, he's my once and former tail, all right, and he looks as jumpy as a flea-infested dog.

I hustle back past the restroom, hearing loud men's voices. I pause before entering the dining room, when suddenly the guy with the bad rug lurches from the booth and makes for the area I just vacated. Bob Fosse couldn't have choreo-graphed this better.

As I pace toward our booth, Marisol's sliding out. She glances up, and I veer toward the kitchen, motioning her to follow. Together, we wind through the steam and sharp food smells and organized chaos, skirting cooks and busboys, and provoking a chorus of complaints. We're almost to the back door, when I hear the door at the front burst open and smash against the wall.

Yep, it's the dynamic duo. They look quite disgruntled.

And, damn, they spot us. They're staring daggers, and rather than have to dodge the real thing, I push Marisol toward the door, saying, "Cut left, go to the street, turn right." Then I grab the dessert wagon I'd seen earlier, fully stacked with scrumptious-looking pastries. I yank it into the passageway and shove it hard toward the advancing men.

Now what?

Chapter 19

The cart rolls straight and true, plowing into the thin man, sending pastries and desserts splattering to the floor, forming a gooey paste on which the bald guy slips and slides like a duck on ice, then goes down hard. I burst out the door and slam it shut. A delivery man's struggling with a hand truck piled high with cardboard cartons, herding it down the metal ramp of a truck parked in the alley. I grab the top box on the pile and pull, toppling several boxes in front of the doorway. There's a crash of glass from within. Yuck, it must be tomato sauce.

As I hoof down the alley, trying to get my numb leg to perform a semblance of jogging, the raucous sounds of rude language and the door smacking repeatedly against the tumbled pile of cartons ring in my ears. I don't see Marisol, so I assume she's made the turn up ahead.

When I reach the sidewalk, I turn the corner, glancing back, and see the two guys now out in the alley, nasty expressions on their pasty faces, setting out in earnest to overtake me. Oddly, one of them is carrying a plastic freezer sack in one hand. He's trying to open it as he runs.

Up ahead about twenty yards I spot Marisol in a slow jog, holding back, her head turned to see if I show up. I motion for her to keep moving, then redouble my efforts to get my bod in gear. I'm checking the car and foot traffic, trying to come up with an idea.

There. "Jump in," I yell.

She peers at me, baffled, but looks toward the street where I'm pointing. She hesitates a moment, then clambers into the rear seat of a horse-drawn carriage that's gliding down the street. A startled middle-aged couple stare at her for a moment, then scoot over to give her room.

I'm almost to the next street corner, and I slow a bit, checking behind me. The guys in the dark suits trot out of the alley, spot me, and slow to a brisk walk. I presume they're trying to overtake me without bringing attention to themselves. I grin and wave at them. Sometimes I wonder what goes through my head.

The skinny guy raises his arm. How nice. At least he's going to be civil and return my greeting. Maybe these guys aren't so bad after all. Maybe I've misread their intentions.

But his arm stops level with my chest. There's something dark in his hand. Gun!

I turn to run, my stiff leg wobbles beneath me, and I stumble, nearly falling, but regain my balance by pressing one hand on the sidewalk, then pushing myself back up to my feet. I don't hear a shot, but something plinks loudly against a speed limit sign beside me.

Tinkles of sound pepper the sidewalk, and I glance down, seeing shards of ice. When I look back at the men, they've stopped in their tracks, the skinny guy doing something with the gun. Looks like he's trying to reload.

I figure that's my cue to bounce.

I take off at a crisper pace than I'd managed before, following the carriage, which has turned at the corner and is now about a third of the way down the block. I catch up to it, hobble in front, and grasp the horse's harness with one hand, rubbing my hand on his velvety nose, and talking to him in a low, soft voice. "Hey, now, old fella. Let's just ease on down the street a bit and I'll owe you a hatful of sugar cubes."

And though the young lady driving the carriage seems shocked, I give her a reassuring smile, and she manages to relax and go with the flow. Then Marisol, the middle-aged tourists, and my new equestrian friend and I proceed down the street as though we owned it. I glance across the horse's withers to see two bewildered-looking guys in cheap suits jogging, slowing, then staring up and down the sidewalk as if they'd just lost the circus elephant.

We turn another corner, I extract Marisol from the carriage, hand the driver a nice wad of cash, then escort my beautiful partner to my waiting SUV. I thought it would be handier parked here than confined in a lot. Luckily, my hunch was right.

Once inside and rolling down the street, feeling safe for the moment, we begin to laugh about the Keystone Kops chase scene. I've got my case binder with its snoopy transmitter and recorder wrapped inside a thick moving pad I keep in the back to kneel on when I change flats. So I'm free to compare notes with Marisol about why we think the two killers might be after us.

"They've got to think you're onto something," I tell her.

"But I don't know anything. I was only helping you on your murder case," she says.

"The skinny guy. He must have suspected you might recognize him, so he came into the restaurant to see."

"But how would he know I was running a trace on the credit card?" she asks.

Chagrined, I tell her about the recorder in my case binder. And I explain how I've probably been duped by the local police agencies I've been working with, which agencies were themselves most likely bamboozled by the big federal agents from NSA, or wherever, telling them some elaborate cover story about why they were checking up on me.

"Which reminds me," I say, turning back up the street where we first horsejacked the carriage, "I need to check something."

"What if those guys are still around?"

A legitimate concern. "Nah, they're probably searching the free Plaza parking lots. I gave them a phony lead over their listening device."

"Won't they figure out you discovered the transmitter?"

"I don't think so. At least, not right away. In fact, I'll get it back out pretty soon. I need to let them think they're still in control."

I wheel in against the curb, jump out, glance up and down the street, then search the ground near where I stumbled and got shot at. There. One sliver on the sidewalk, and another couple in the gutter. I gently slip them into one of the plastic baggies I keep in my pocket.

"What's that?" Marisol asks as I clamber back inside my SUV with my prize packet.

"Pieces of dry ice."

"You came back for dry ice?"

"But, of course, there's a method to my—"

"Max, let's get out of here."

Good idea. I press the pedal and wheel back into the street.

Once we make a few turns and begin to pick up speed with the flow of traffic, Marisol regards me again and says, "Now you can impress me with your crafty reasons for acting crazy."

Rather a backhanded compliment. "I think these slivers were part of a dart. The guy shot it at me from a CO_2 gun. I'm betting the lab will find these pieces impregnated with curare."

"*Dios mio*, what's that all about?"

"Probably what they used to shoot Kyle Mossler. Oh, grab that small cooler on the floor behind your seat."

She does, then I place the baggie inside and close it up.

"Will that preserve the pieces?" she asks.

"No, they'll still sublimate, but maybe we can contain the liquid curare."

She's shaking her head, looking stunned. "Max, what are we up against here?"

"These are no street punks. They're with some organization. But we need to figure out just exactly who they are, what their mission is, and whether they're trying to kill us."

"They tried to shoot you with a poison dart. What do you think?"

I stare at her, crack a grin, then start to laugh, building louder and louder until I'm chortling so gut-wrenchingly hard that I just miss a young jaywalker who's stepped into my path. He's heavily impaled with silver ornaments through his ears, nose, and lower lip. Though startled by his brush with death, he manages to flash me a hand signal flaunting his IQ.

"Where to now?" Marisol asks, a touch of despair in her voice.

"Hillsboro. Then we'll stop at a Wal-Mart and buy you some extra clothes."

"You don't like my wardrobe?" she says, sounding miffed.

"I didn't mean to insult you. Just thought you'd want some casual clothes for hanging around at my place."

"What do you mean? I've got to get back to D.C."

"Not until we've solved this case. I want you where I can try to protect you."

She protests, but eventually gives in. Says she'll stay a few days, anyway. I sure hope that's enough.

As I drive, Marisol and I rehearse our script a bit, then I pull over and extract the binder from the thick blanket that's covering it, saying as I do, ". . . so it's a good thing I gave you the key to my SUV and you got it out of the lot before those guys caught up to me."

"You always did move slow, *cunado*. Anyway, why do you think they were after you?"

"Not for my money, that's for sure," I say.

"You know, Max, the slim guy looked vaguely familiar to me, but I can't place him. Do you know these guys?"

"Can't say for sure," I say. "The skinny guy kept eye-balling me. Could've been someone I arrested once."

"That's why we hightailed it out the back?"

"I like to play it safe. One time the brother of a guy I put away tried to slip a pipe bomb in my mailbox."

"Well, this guy took a shot at you. So what are you going to do?"

I slow at the toll booth where I grab a turnpike ticket then zoom ahead.

"I didn't get a good enough look at them to give the cops a description. I'm not going to spend the evening at the station for nothing."

"Max, you can't just let this go."

"Let's go back to my place. I'll think about it overnight. Right now, I'm whipped."

"That's it," says Carl, cutting the wheel of the black Honda to the left, changing lanes. "We can catch the turnpike up ahead. Won't be far behind them."

"Rather convenient, don't you think, Carl?"

Carl looks at him in wonderment. "What?"

"How we suddenly pick up the voice recording? After it's been off for a half hour?"

"Jesus, Bones, what is it with you? What's wrong now?" In a huff, he signals, then takes the exit to I-70 West.

Scratching at the edge of his hairpiece, Bones shakes his head and frowns. "I'm just glad we've got our trump card working. I'm not sure I trust what Mr. Austin says anymore."

Chapter 20

Some forty-five minutes later we roll into Hillsboro, I pay the toll, then exit at Burlingame Road. Turn right, drive a few blocks, then take another right at 37th Street. Roll along for several minutes, flipping on my lights as I drive, then I turn into the parking lot of a local Wal-Mart.

"I thought you were kidding," Marisol says.

"We're not going to a fashion show."

"Good thing."

"Hey, you look great in anything—dressy, casual, whatever."

"You think I'm gonna fall for *that* line?"

Thought it was worth a try. "We can look, anyway."

She shrugs her shoulders and points at the binder with the recorder.

"What say we stop here and grab a bite?" I say. "My stomach's wondering why dinner got interrupted."

"I don't think I can eat, but I'll have some coffee."

"Deal. Here we are." That should buy us an hour.

I watch Marisol exit the dressing room for the fifth or so time, wearing another pair of jeans. She's tried on various pairs of slacks, too, and several different tops. Have to admit she's like a supermodel; whatever she wears looks like a fine fashion statement.

"I think that's enough for now, Max. I can't stay more

than a couple of days at most."

I nod. "Let's get you some boots."

Her eyes widen. "What on earth—"

"Come on, they're comfortable. I wear them all the time."

"But why do I need . . ."

I'm already moving in that direction, so she scoops up the pants and tops and follows. "Here we go," I say, stopping at a display featuring Justin cowboy boots.

She gives me a sideways look. "Are you pulling something—"

"Tug these on. Here, let me get you some cotton socks."

She's seated with one shoe off and several boxes around her on the floor. I toss her the socks, which she catches with one hand. Tomboy.

"Why do I need boots? There's something you're not telling me."

"There's lots of things I never tell you, dear, but just trust me on this one. It'll be fine."

"You know I never trust men. That's how I've kept from getting my heart broken."

" 'Better to have loved and lost,' they say."

"No, it's better to have avoided ugly entanglements." She's eyeing me sharply.

"Listen, it might snow again. These kicks will be handy. Plus, it can get muddy."

"But I'll be in D.C. I can't hang around here forever while you try to put this case together."

"I'm betting you're the one who'll solve it."

She's standing now, with one boot on. And she shoots me a look that's sharper and faster than Skeleton Man's dry ice dart. "How would I do that?"

"With your lovely, supple fingers and your prodigious brain, of course. The answers must be hiding in a computer somewhere. All we need is to access them."

"Which you have no idea how to do." She leans down and tugs on the other boot, showing cleavage that turns my brain to mush.

"You got it. Good thing I've got the world's best expert working with me."

"No way, Max. I'm not bad, but if we're up against some heavyweights, which I think we are, I don't stand a chance."

"You always did underestimate yourself."

"Hmmm. Well, what do you think?" she says, turning her foot one way, then the other.

"Those boots are you all over. Let's take this stuff and go. We've got places to be and people to find."

"There they are," says Bones.

Carl nods, rubbing his pate. "Guess you were right."

"Yeah, it's a good thing we stuck that homing device on Austin's ride. He's trickier than I'd expected."

"So should we pop him now?"

Sighing, Bones watches the couple slide into the Trailblazer. "Not here in town. I want to catch him outside Hillsboro if we can, so it won't be connected with the kid we hit."

"You said no one knows anything, anyway."

"That's right, Carl. I don't think anyone's onto us, we're well-covered, but I don't want to get stuff stirred up again."

"What about the gal?" Carl says, firing up the Chevy and pulling out of the lot, trailing the bright red truck.

"I don't know. You think she recognized me?"

"I don't think she saw you from close enough, Bones. Plus, she was running away."

"Well, hell, where are they headed now? I thought they'd go to his place."

"Maybe he's getting her a room someplace."

"Then he's a bigger idiot than I thought."

"Aren't we going toward town?" Marisol asks.

"Sort of."

"But why? We're not going to your house?"

"We need to pick up some stuff to help us out in this case."

"What could we possibly do? We don't know who these guys are or how to figure out what they're doing. Other than killing people."

"People involved with Zipdata."

"So?"

I reach into my jacket pocket, grab the CD I got from Damian Roberts's dad, and hand it to Marisol. She takes it as though it's covered with the Ebola virus. "What's this?"

"I'm hoping it's the Rosetta Stone for unraveling this enigma."

"But I'm no archaeologist."

"Then this is your big chance to dig up a bone."

She mutters something I don't catch. I don't think I'll ask her to repeat it.

I pull off Wanamaker into the parking lot of Best Buy.

"What now?" she asks.

"I thought we'd pick up a computer."

"Don't you have one at home?"

"Probably not powerful enough for a pro like you. Besides, I'm not taking you there. It's too dangerous."

"Then what?"

I pull into a space and kill the motor. "Let's go see what we can find."

After twenty minutes of shopping, we've got a system assembled that Marisol seems comfortable with and I can almost afford.

As we check out, she says, "Now I'm getting hungry."

"There's a ton of joints around here," I say, and name some for her.

She picks the Amarillo Steak House, a spot I like for their food and casual ambience. Reminds me of the places I frequented when I lived in Texas. As we walk in, I curse the city council under my breath for not having the guts to declare Hillsboro's restaurants smoke-free.

"Something?" Marisol says.

"Kind of smoky."

"Won't do more than coat your lungs with noxious, poisonous chemicals."

"Since you put it that way."

We sit, order a couple of cold brain benders, and study the younger couples gathered throughout the place, most looking like they're dating.

"You going out with anyone?" Marisol asks.

"Not to speak of. How about you?"

She fiddles with her glass of water. "There was a guy I thought about getting serious with last year. We got along pretty well."

"But?"

"Hard to say. He didn't have that special quality I'm looking for."

"What's that?" I say, wondering if I do.

"Sort of a mix of intelligence, wit, charm. I don't know. Just a way of looking at the world and interacting with people."

"Was he with the Bureau?"

"Yeah, maybe that was the problem."

"There are lots of nice guys in the outfit."

The pleasant waitress approaches and sets down our bottles of Coors Lite and a couple of mugs. Um-mmm.

We pour, then look at each other. I lift my mug. "To the future."

She nods. "With fond memories of the past."

"That, too." I take a big gulp. Smooth.

"You think you'll remarry?" She takes a sip of her brew.

I almost choke on the beer I'm swallowing. "Couldn't really tell you. That's about as remote in my thoughts as Sirius."

"What's that?"

"A faraway star."

"So, there's no chance?"

"Well, you have to consider that it's the brightest star in the heavens."

"Which means?"

"That I have no idea. Same as with anything else in my life."

"Somehow I think you're more self-directed than that."

"There is a time to every season under heaven. So maybe that will crop up in my future. It just seems too soon to think about."

"I understand. I'm sort of in the same position."

"No, you're like Hoover was. Married to the FBI."

She takes a large swallow of her suds. "God, I hope you're wrong about that. But I'm not sure, one way or the other."

"My predictions of the future hold at about fifty-fifty. So don't get overly concerned. Monkeys do as well."

"Then maybe we ought to hire one to help on your project."

"Nah, I figure if we get in a bind, the cows can help."

"The cows?"

"Let's order, and I'll tell you about it."

Chapter 21

"Why are we on the interstate, Max?"

I glance at Marisol, pat her leg, then blow out a breath. "I want you to be safe. But you need some space to work, too."

"And?"

"Sharon's dad has a ranch northwest of Hillsboro."

"A *ranch?* You're taking me to a *ranch?*"

"Hey, you're in Kansas. Besides, it's the safest place I can think of. There's a suite of rooms under the main house. You can set up the computer there. Plenty of room to work, and it's got a fridge, stove, bedrooms. I'll even throw in all the steak you can eat."

"Is this house in the middle of a herd of cows?"

"Don't worry, they're out to pasture. The ranch house is for people. There's a foreman and a ranch hand on site who can protect you, and, besides, no one would ever think to look for you there."

"But what about you?"

"I've got more leads to run out. I figure if I stay on the move and watch my step, I'll be fine. Meanwhile, I'd like for you to figure out what we're up against."

"That's a big order, Max."

"No step for a stepper like you."

"Your confidence is way overblown. But let me check something."

As she pulls her phone from her purse, I angle off the expressway. There are just two-lane roads the rest of the way. That's good for watching for a tail.

"See him, Carl?"

"Yeah, I got it."

"Don't run up on him."

"No need. The transmitter working okay?"

"Yeah, I'm getting a strong signal. You can stay way back. Not much traffic out here."

"Wonder where he's going?"

"He's got me stumped this time."

"Now I feel better about this project," says Marisol, staring at her cell phone.

"How come?"

"We caught a break. John just answered me about that guy who rented the van at the airport. We got a hit."

"You're kidding."

"No *chiste,* man. It was a true name. Carl Crabtree. Got his description, where he lives, where his wife spends his paycheck, the whole bit."

"And where he works?"

"U.S. Government. The agency wasn't specified."

"I'll be damned."

"Probably the same agency as the skinny guy, whatever that is."

"But why would his name come up, but not that of Bones?"

"He probably skipped a step he should've done to keep his name out of the records."

Sounds like a mistake I'd make. "So why the hell would they be murdering innocent kids?"

"Maybe the kids weren't that innocent."

I think back to David's description of Kyle Mossler as a cracker and phreaker, with the mention of him inserting a Trojan horse into a security program.

"What're you thinking, Max?"

I tell her, with the caveat, "But we're getting into uncharted territory with that. I haven't checked out anything along those lines."

Marisol waggles the CD in her hand. "Maybe this will give us the directions we need to wade into that murky water."

She seems more enthusiastic now. But somehow, I feel depressed. I'm not sure I like where this may be going. "Could be," is all I say.

"What's this little town?"

"St. Mary's. We'll grab some groceries here."

Before she can protest, I stop and get out. She reluctantly follows. Most of the stuff she picks out from the shelves and bins and coolers is vegetables and greens. No wonder she stays so slim.

Back in the Trailblazer, leaving town, I say, "The ranch is a little to the north, in the Flint Hills. It's beautiful during the day."

"And dark as pitch at night, I'll bet."

"The better to see the endless stars."

"You'd better keep your head out of the clouds for a while, Max. At least until we figure out what these guys are up to." She's shaking her head in reproof, but she's got a hint of a smile that makes her dimples look as cute as angel's footprints.

"Current theory is that dark matter and dark energy make up most of the Universe. If we don't explore that, we can't understand the workings of the light parts."

"So you're going to unlock the secrets of the Universe?"

"Maybe the criminal universe. At least this small one. As

you know, there may be an infinite number of parallel universes."

"I didn't know that, and I don't really want to think about it. That gives me chills. It's hard enough just getting along on this little planet."

She's right about that. Don't guess I'll mention how tenuous our position is, with ninety percent of the asteroids that could wipe out the Earth totally uncharted and unknown to our scientists. So, I say, "I'm still trying to figure that out, too."

In a few minutes I turn onto another blacktop road.

"Are we almost there?" she says.

"Couple of miles. You're in ranch country, honey."

She manages a half smile. "Swell, partner."

After an hour or so I get her settled. Clothes in the dresser drawers, clean sheets on the bed, grub in the fridge. Computer up and running.

"So now what?" she says.

"Come here," I say, then move into her and give her a warm hug. "I've got to leave you now, but I'll keep in touch. You've got my cell phone number."

"Which you turn off all the time."

"I'll keep it on. Promise."

"What if there's nothing on this CD?" she says.

"Then we're back to square one. Maybe you can do some more traces on Carl and the skinny dude—Bones. Anyway, I've still got a couple of things to look into."

"And who'll watch your back?" She looks very concerned. I'd like to smooth those wrinkles on her forehead.

"Binga. And Jeff. I'll contact him when I get back to town."

"That detective whose son got arrested?"

"That's him. He'll keep an eye out for me."

"I have a bad feeling about this, Max."

"Don't be trusting those superstitious vibes of yours." Which, unfortunately in this instance, may prove to be accurate. "We're dealing with scientific stuff now. Once we figure out what they're doing, we'll probably know why they're killing people to protect it. And we've already got names for the bad guys. That'll help a lot."

"Maybe. But I've been wondering, how do you always get mixed up in stuff like this?"

I think of my quiet life in the country. Isolated. Removed from the busy world. "Marisol, I haven't got a clue. Got to go. Keep in touch."

"What do you think they did there?" Carl says.

"Beats me, but the lights are still on in the lower part of the house. And here comes his truck."

"Should I follow him?"

"Hell, yes. But stay way back, or he'll spot us. There's no one else out here but a bunch of cows and buzzards."

The trip back to Hillsboro seems twice as long. I miss Marisol's company—she's a very pleasant companion. Not to mention nice to look at and wonderful to smell.

I check my rearview mirror. There's a car back there a mile or so. Is he on me? I can't tell. Probably not.

Once back in town, I turn into the parking lot for Sam's Club, stop, and watch the cars pulling in behind me. There's nothing that looks suspicious. No huge bald guys or skinny ones with hawk-like faces and bad hairpieces.

So, I unwrap the moving pad from the binder with the recorder and say, "Here it is, Marisol. It's not the Ritz, but you'll be comfortable here for a couple of days. Then I'll get you back to D.C., I promise." Next, I open the car door and slam it. Do it again. I sit quietly for a few minutes. Open the door and shut it once more. Then start up my ride and head for home.

I'm feeling drained. Exhausted. Whipped.

Still, it'll be good to see Binga and to get to bed early. Tomorrow will be a busy day. If I see tomorrow.

Sunrays light up my mini-blinds, and when I hear Binga's cavernous snoring in the corner, it hits me that we've survived the night intact. I've learned to be thankful for small blessings. In this case, perhaps it's a big one.

I hate to call Marisol so early, but I can't help it. I have to know if she's all right. By the fifth ring, I'm getting anxious.

"H'lo." Sleepy voice.

"It's me. You all right?"

"I guess so. I'm still wondering where I am and who'd be calling me in the middle of the night."

"C'mon, you're used to that." Everyone in the Bureau is.

"But I'm not usually stuck in the middle of nowhere."

"You kidding? You're in God's country. Everywhere else is nowhere."

"Omygod. There are some cows outside the window."

"Look closer. See the barbed wire fence? They can't get you."

"Oh, yeah. I see it. That's okay, then."

"Besides, they eat grass."

"But they step on people. And poke you with their horns. I've seen some Westerns."

"Not if you're nice to them."

"I don't know how to be nice to a cow."

I chuckle under my breath. "Think of them as big teddy bears. Only not as bright."

"That's very comforting."

"You sleep okay, Marisol?"

"Pretty good. At first, I couldn't get used to all the quiet. Then I realized there are other sounds besides traffic. The wind, cows lowing, a train rolling in the distance."

"You're getting acclimated, cowgirl."

"Maybe. You at home?"

"Right. I'm going to the PD, then maybe out of town."

"Don't tell me where. Just in case."

"Fair enough. Get some coffee and get to work. I didn't mean for you to take a vacation. That's no dude ranch, you know."

"Real funny. I'm a beach bunny, not a hayseed. Get someone else to ride the prairies with you, bub."

"You ever been on a horse, dear?"

"A few times. I had an uncle with a farm in Alabama that I visited when I was a kid. He'd always put me on one of his nags. He thought I'd like it. But I was more at home on a surfboard."

"But 'when in Rome . . .' "

"I know. Talk with you later."

"If I come up with anything else, I'll call. You do the same."

"I will, Max. And take care, will you?"

"Always."

I look at the dead phone for a moment, wishing we could talk under more normal conditions. But now is not the time. As Gilda Radner used to say, "It's always something."

I punch in the number for the PD and get Jeff Bagley on the phone.

"So what's going on, Max? Any new leads?"

"I'm coming down there in an hour. I'll fill you in then. Anything new on your end?"

"Nah, they've snowed me with some other cases and told

me that Arty and Hal can work the Mossler murder. Something about how I'm too close to it, anyway."

Perhaps that's right. But, still. Seems he has a big stake in it.

"Okay, I'll see you soon."

"How long we gonna keep followin' him?"

Bones gets a stony look and says, "What do you think?"

"Until he gives up on the case or we take him out?"

Nodding. "Something like that. You got something better to do?"

"I'm just ready to go home."

"But this is urgent, right?"

Drumming the steering wheel, then accelerating after the Trailblazer, Carl says, "Looks like he's going to the PD again."

"That's good. He won't learn anything there."

Chapter 22

I manage to get Jeff alone in his office at the PD. The usual chaos reigns throughout the area. In a low voice, I ask, "Could we talk somewhere private, Jeff?"

He studies me for a long moment. "Sure, let's check the interview rooms."

"Not the one with the mirror."

"No way."

Jeff peeks inside a small, empty room. "Here we go." He flips on the light and settles into a chair as I drop into another one across from him, the dull gray interview table between us.

I've got to make a decision. Can I trust Jeff enough to tell him what I think I know about what's going on in this case? Will he help me, or join the other guys in tying a noose around my stuck-out neck?

"So what's up?" he asks.

What the heck. Here goes nothing. "I needed to pick up your interview report on Will Tanger and touch base with you on whatever else you've found."

"Fair enough. But as I said . . ." He wipes a big paw across his mouth and frowns.

"What?"

"I'm really out of the loop on this now. I mean, I'm not actively working it. And I don't think Arty and Hal are doing much, either. I was hoping you'd come up with something."

For a big bear of a guy, Jeff can have soulful eyes. And you have to trust someone like that. "I'm making some headway, Jeff. I won't tell you everything right now, because some things need to be checked out further."

"But you'll tell me that David's not involved?"

"I'm pretty sure of that. Hey, you knew that anyway."

He nods, looking grim, then gives me a smile. "But hearing it from a pro like you makes my day."

"I still want you and David to watch your backs. This may not be over yet."

"And who's watching yours?"

"Take a glance at it whenever you can. And I've got some Bureau folks helping me."

"What else can I do?"

I was hoping he'd ask that. "Let's get those reports. Then I'd like to ask a favor."

We slip out the side entrance and into Jeff's car. About ten blocks away, near the expressway, we pull up to a large out-door parking area, ringed by a link fence topped with barbed wire—the police impound lot. Once inside the gate, we park beside a long row of forlorn-looking cars, most of them with dings, faded paint, and even cracked windshields. Looks like a last repository for consummate losers in the automotive world.

"Those are the ones we're using for surveillance now," Jeff says, pointing at a dozen vehicles of all types parked toward the side, away from the street.

"Couple of vans," I say.

"Right."

A plain tan one and a light blue one. "Do you ever repaint these?"

"Sure, sometimes. Or we'll tag them differently. We'll even use different logos or signs on the sides."

That's what I thought. "Where do you keep the signs?"

"In there." He nods toward a metal-sided building fifty yards away. "Want to see 'em?"

"More than anything."

He squints at me oddly, but starts walking, and as we make our way across the lot, I get a tingling sensation on the back of my neck. Sometimes small breaks are all you need in very big cases to crack the whole thing wide open.

We nod at a guy stationed at the front of the place, then approach a tall gray oversized storage locker at the rear of the room. Jeff works the hefty combination lock, opens it, and rummages on a shelf about waist-high, pulling out some magnetized vinyl signs advertising various phony business names, city offices, or whatever the cops could think of to stick on the side of the vans to make them fit in wherever they were doing a surveillance.

ACE PLUMBERS in bold blue letters. Black's Lock Shop in green letters, with the outline of a key beneath. Fancy Florist Shoppe in pink script with some roses drawn to the side. Pretty authentic-looking.

Then the one I was hoping to find: Saxton Carpets in red script. Fits what Pete Sanders's neighbor, Sheri, told me she saw on the white van. "Is there a checkout log for these?"

"Nah, whoever needs 'em just takes one. 'Course the vehicles are charged out. You need to check that?"

"No, I already found the van. Come on, I need to fill you in on some things."

We stop at The Classic Bean, an espresso place I like for its casual atmosphere, with old wood floors and a high ceiling, tables and chairs scattered about, and wonderful scents filling the air. We sit down to sip some fine coffee and discuss what I've learned in the case. At least, locally. I don't tell Jeff that I suspect federal agents may be involved.

"You're making progress, then. Think you can track the shooters from the credit cards?"

"We're working on that."

If Jeff seems aware of complicity between his department and the feds, I'll have to change my game plan, but so far, he seems in the dark.

"Let me know if I can help nail them."

"You know I always count on you to bail me out."

He waves it away. "I was in the right spot one time. Big deal."

"Big enough that I'm still able to collect my pension and contemplate the Cosmos."

"First things first, I notice."

"Takes beans to stimulate the brain."

"If that were true," he says, patting his belly, "I'd be the smartest guy in the Universe. This one, anyway."

"So you subscribe to the multiple universe theory?"

"Hell, I don't follow any of that gobbledy gook, Max. I'm just trying to impress you."

"Big guy, you always do."

I ride back to the PD with Jeff, sneaking in the side door and exiting the front where I get into my Trailblazer. I'm sure I have a tail, but I don't spot them right now. I drive away, then after a few blocks, I park next to the YMCA to review the reports Bagley gave me.

As I finish reading the write-up of the interview of Will Tanger, the Texas kid who was supposed to be an expert in encryption in the Zipdata corporation, I have to conclude that Jeff was right: the kid was very tight-lipped about what the company was doing. And, of course, at the time of the interview, no one realized the importance of a security program that was sold to government agencies, so nothing was said about that.

My cell phone goes off. "Yes?"

"Hey, Sunshine. You having a bad day?"

"Yo, Marisol. No, you just caught me speculating about something."

"Something good?"

"Maybe. What's shaking with you?"

"John just scanned me a driver's license photo of the guy with the credit card who rented the van. Carl Crabtree looks to me like our bald friend from the restaurant."

"Then we're on the right track. Now we need to find out what they're angry about or scared of."

"Learn anything new at the PD?"

"I think there's some cooperation between those federal agents and our local officials. At least, at the higher levels. The detectives may not realize what's going on."

"What about the Denver cops?"

"Probably the same setup there."

"And other federal agencies?"

"That's what we need to find out, dear."

"I was afraid you'd say that."

"I'll see you in a couple of hours."

"I'm the one without horns."

"I can spot you a mile away." She's always a stand-out. In any kind of herd.

And now for one last try with my buddy, Pete Sanders.

He's not there. Garage door up, 4Runner gone. Hopefully, just on a trip to the store.

I could wait here for him. Or not. I circle the block and park at a spot where the house looks vacant, with a FOR SALE sign in the yard. Out of my truck, I study the house a minute, as though I'm a prospective buyer, then walk around the corner, down the street, and slip down the side of Sanders's house.

Sliding patio doors at the back. They're not quite closed. Tempting, and it's not like I'm going to take anything.

I slip inside, calling Pete's name. All quiet. That's good.

Now down the hallway to his office. Lights still on, computer up and running. I find a plastic container filled with CDs. Flipping through them now, my heart's thumping hard, ears alert for sounds of any activity.

They're labeled: Bank records. Tax info. Credit card purchases. Zipdata corporate structure. Zipdata programs. Zipdata contracts.

I slip in the one labeled "contracts," and bring it up. Not a whole lot of entries, but there's some pretty big numbers involved. I look for recent ones about the Securegard program.

There. Sold four months ago to two medium-size civilian corporations. A couple of weeks after that to the National Security Agency. Then a few weeks later to the Department of Containment, U.S. Government. What the hell? I'm familiar with NSA, but I've never heard of a Department of Containment. It's got an address listed in D.C.

I print out the page, then check the other two CDs. One lists several programs concerning some scientific projects with descriptions I find hard to follow. I print those out, then turn to the CD on corporate structure.

It shows the six members of the corporation, with a description of their specialties and various strengths in the computer field, mathematics, physics, etc. There are some other people listed with phone numbers beside them, each with a sentence or two as to their background and work specialty, probably consultants for the corporation. I hit the print button again, and the machine whirs into action.

A squeal outside. The driveway? Yes, there's a car door slamming.

I eject the CD and slip it back into the case. Grab the

pages from the printer. Head for the patio door and slip out as I hear the front door opening.

My nerve endings feel fried. I duck as I pass by the windows, then turn on to the sidewalk and hurry back to my getaway car. I'd never make a good burglar, I'm way too jumpy.

And what did I gain by that, anyway? Maybe more than by talking to Sanders, which I can always do later. Let's see if these clues rocket me to alien places.

Chapter 23

"You're going *where?*" Marisol says, her mouth full of lettuce.

"You know, The Alamo City. I need to talk with that other kid in Zipdata, Will Tanger." I cut off a tender bite of steak, blood and juices running beneath my knife.

"And leave me here alone in the wilderness?" She swallows the greenery, then knocks off a big gulp of a long-neck Corona. Her dark eyes seem to flash, but maybe it's just a reflection from the candle flickering on the table between us.

"Dear, you're in God's country. The great outdoors—with fresh, clean air beneath a huge blue sky. Relax and enjoy."

"Just me and the smelly cows," she pouts.

"Take a break from the computer," I say. "Saddle up one of the horses and go for a ride. You'll appreciate the place more."

"What if I break a leg?"

"The horse will come back to the stable."

"With or without me?"

I shrug, stifle a grin, and follow the bite of steak I just swallowed with a couple of gulps of pure Rocky Mountain spring water laced with alcohol—a heavenly, cold Coors Lite. "If he comes back without you, Brand will go looking for you. Besides, those horses are broke, you won't get bucked."

"Is your ranch hand really named Brand?"

"Jack Brand. Everyone calls him—"

"Yeah, yeah. So he finds me crumpled up in the pasture and ropes me by the leg and drags me back to the bunkhouse?"

"You've watched too many bad Westerns."

"Whatever. *Hijo de*—"

"Whoa, listen, I'll saddle up one of the horses for you before I leave in the morning."

"I can do it. If I get desperate."

I shrug. "You could just go for a walk. Enjoy the day. Supposed to be sunny and warmer tomorrow."

She picks at the salad with her fork, eyeing the steak platter.

"Want a piece?" I offer.

"Yes, damn it. Give me a couple of bites."

I cut off a tender end piece. Sirloin. Mouth-watering good.

She glances at me, then digs in, chewing like a ranch hand with a plug of Red Man in her jaw. "This is really good," she says. *"Muy sabroso."*

"I know. Want some more?"

"Just a little."

I cut another piece and fork it over to her plate. "You haven't told me what miracles you worked with the computer today."

She gives me what could only be called a mischievous grin. "I thought you'd never ask. The CD you gave me had stuff about the Securegard program."

"Such as?"

"A catalogue-type description of what it does, plus the names of the corporations and government agencies Zipdata sold it to."

"Perhaps NSA and the Department of Containment?"

Now her mouth drops open. "How'd you find that out?"

"I don't want you to have guilty knowledge. Have you heard of that Containment bunch?"

"As you know, we're awash in departments and agencies in D.C., but I don't recall that one."

"Me either. Can you check the address?"

She makes a note. "I'll have John check it out."

"Did you do any more work on Crabtree?"

"Actually, that's the kicker I came up with," she says with a smile. "In one of his credit card files he listed the same address as the Department of Containment for his work address."

"So maybe we're getting somewhere," I say hopefully.

"Or maybe it'll all wash out," she says.

"You're always dashing my hopes and dreams."

"You mean your *fantasias*."

As the jet veers toward the south, gaining altitude, hopefully with Texas on its radar, I study the various green and brown tracts of land, curling blue ribbons of water, and pale streaks of concrete highways laid across the outskirts of Kansas City. Fantasies, Marisol said. Maybe so. But she always did inspire such thoughts in me. And I can't tell if she's blowing me off or just being playful.

I suppose time will tell.

Just as I hope Will Tanger will tell me something to help bring this case into focus. But why wouldn't he have been more helpful during his initial interview? Or maybe at that point Jeff didn't know what questions to ask.

I used to work in San Antonio, and I always liked the town. Great Mexican food, lots of fun activities, warm weather. In fact, you need access to a swimming pool or two in order to survive there. And a good lawn mower, as you have to cut grass about ten months out of the year. But Texans do love their parties, which can be rip-roaring fun.

During the flight, the two teenage girls seated next to me whisper to each other and giggle the whole time. So, I page through my notes and the typed interviews I've done and the ones conducted by the Hillsboro and Denver PDs, trying to get an overview. And I think back about everything I've heard, thought, and speculated during the case.

Consider the two mysterious figures who killed Kyle Mossler. They're likely the same guys that were trailing me, who later came after Marisol and me at the restaurant. But why are they involved? What's their motive in this scenario? And what's their ultimate goal?

They've eliminated some of the members of Zipdata, but not others. Are they just biding their time? Are the others on the list?

And what about Marisol and me? Maybe John and other FBI agents. Maybe Jeff. Are we in line to be exterminated because we know something may be going on?

I study the binder. I brought it with me to let "the listeners" know I'm going to San Antonio, but I said nothing specific soon enough for them to catch the same flight. Also, I need to keep them away from Marisol. Hopefully, they don't know where she is. Maybe I should have gotten her a bodyguard. But, sometimes, the fewer people that know what's going on, the better.

I've learned it's hard to know who to trust in this case.

Just as we might not know about the asteroid that'll cross Earth's path until it's too late. Much like a stranger stepping out of a dark alley. With an air gun in his hand loaded with a poisonous dart.

But I'm giving myself chills. I sound like a Stephen King novel. Bummer.

Thinking more positively, I decide that if I can crack the

Tanger kid, we might have a good chance to put the pieces together and solve this deep, dark enigma. So I plan my interview strategy. Decide what I know, what I contemplate, what I need to know. Weave it all together into a basketful of questions that'll keep him off balance, wondering what information I have, maybe causing him to slip and tell me more than he intended.

The captain comes on the intercom, announcing our imminent arrival to San Antonio International Airport. I suppose the boys in the dark suits will be on the next flight here, trailing me. But I should have plenty of time to do what I need.

The seatbelt sign goes out. I grab my case from the overhead bin and proceed at a snail's pace down the aisle, helping several women extract gigantic bags from the bin along the way. Finally, I smile at the captain and thank him, then emerge from the plane, and head down the walkway.

There's no one in the eager-looking crowd meeting the plane that I recognize. I glance behind me. No one's taking any apparent interest in me. No bald guy. No skinny guy with a ferret face.

As in the pursuit of astronomy, things are looking up.

I park my rental car, a blue Dodge, in a visitor's space at the large apartment complex where Will Tanger lives. Nice digs. Lots of shrubbery, probably flowering in warmer months, with mostly shiny, newer vehicles parked about, many of them SUVs, which these people need about as much as I need a Humvee.

I find Tanger's apartment, but no vehicle is in his assigned parking spot. I pass by the mail boxes, noticing through the slot on his box that he hasn't picked up his mail today, and it's one o'clock now. I pause by his door, hearing nothing, then knock, but there's no answer, no shuffling going on inside, no TV or radio noise. I knock again. Still nothing.

Retreating to my car, I look up his number in my folder, wait a couple of minutes, then call him. It rings four times, then his answering machine picks up. According to the beeps, mine would be the sixth message, but I hang up. Hmmm.

This doesn't bode well. Of course, he might just be buying groceries. Or beer. Or whatever a kid who works from his home does when he gets bored. I hope he hasn't left town.

I slip out of my ride and head back for his apartment. Knock again, hard. Then I get an idea, and I announce to the door, "Hey, Will, it's Uncle Max. You in there, kid?"

I see a curtain move an inch in an adjacent apartment window. Flash of long brown hair. Stuffing my hands in my pockets, I give a nonplussed look to my secret audience.

Then I walk over to her door and knock. Hesitation. Then the door opens to the limit of a short chain. "Yes?" she says in a small voice.

"Hi, young lady, I'm sorry to bother you, I just wondered if you knew Will that lives next door to you there?"

"I know him to say hi to. We talk, sometimes."

"Good, good, I'm his uncle, just dropped by from Austin. He doesn't seem to be in. Do you know where he went and when he'll be back?"

She removes the chain and opens the door about a foot. Lucky Will. She's a very pretty neighbor. "I really don't know. He works at home, so he comes and goes during the day. But you know . . ."

She's thinking. I nod encouragement.

"I put some trash out at . . . oh, about eleven, and his car wasn't here."

"But you don't know where he may have gone?"

"Not really." She brushes back a wisp of hair that's fallen

across her face. She has huge blue eyes.

"Does he still drive that Mustang?" I'm totally fishing.

"Oh, no. He's got a new 'Vette. A red one."

"Man. That's Will, all right. Probably got a vanity tag, too."

She laughs. "I slammed him about that when he got it. ZIPPY1. Can you believe it?"

"Too much," I say. "Would you know any places around here he might hang out during the day or evening?"

"There's a lounge half a mile from here. Then the strip of clubs over by 410 and McAlister, you know them?"

"Sure. Anywhere else?"

"Could check the miniplexes at the malls. He's big into movies."

"Thanks for the help. Hope I catch him."

"Want me to tell him you were here?"

"Nah, I'll leave a card in his door."

Chapter 24

I start looking for Tanger at a neighborhood cocktail lounge with a nautical theme—weathered pilings skirting the walkways, lashed together loosely by thick, graying rope, and a large carved pelican roosted beside the entrance—but I spot no red Corvette parked in the lot. The first two clubs on the strip that the girl suggested are also negative. But at the third joint, I see the Vette with the ZIPPY1 tag. She's right, it looks dorky.

I sidle in the door, pause to let my eyes adjust to the dim, smoky atmosphere, then check out the assembled drinkers, pool shooters, and music fans. You have to really love "music," or subtle sounds such as car crashes or metal garbage can lids being banged together, to appreciate the din of the garbled rap tune blaring from four huge speakers hung from the ceiling. If I had a hearing aid, I'd smash it.

There's a bunch of young guys at the bar, all very rowdy, some of whom must have fake IDs which enable them to booze it up. A table of attractive young women is watching them appreciatively, but not so obviously that the kids pick up the signals. There's also a group of middle-aged guys hunkered down in their chairs at the end of the bar, wearing loud sports coats, their ties appropriately at half mast, smoking, and drinking doubles with practiced precision.

Along one wall are groupings of guys and girls who look not much more comfortable than I feel in this raucous, bawdy atmosphere. Some girls who are overweight, underweight,

184

cosmetically challenged. Some guys whose clothes, phy-
siques, and bearings suggest they're not accustomed to the
successful accomplishment of the legendary one-night
stands.

I think I see Tanger. Skinny kid with a pallid complexion.
And as I approach him, I can see he has the red hair and thick
glasses I recall.

"Hi, Will," I say.

He starts to smile, then a worried look crosses his face. He
fidgets with his hands, looking like he's about to bolt from his
chair at the small table. "Uh, do I know you?" he says.

"We never met, but I saw you at Kyle Mossler's funeral.
I'm a friend of David Bagley and his dad."

Now he looks relieved. I wonder why. "Are you the FBI
guy?"

"Yes, retired. But I'm working the case. Could I sit
down?"

He glances around the room. "Uh, sure. Help yourself."

"Are you looking for someone?"

"I . . . well, not really." He fidgets with his glass of beer
and squirms in his seat. I don't know why he's so uncomfort-
able.

"What's wrong, Will?"

He takes a drink. Looks toward the door, then back at me,
sighs, and seems to wilt in his seat. "I'm scared, Mr. Austin."

I wait for more, but it seems he's withdrawing again. "I
see. But just call me Max. I'm your best friend in this matter,
Will. You can trust me."

He stares at me. I think he wants to believe it.

"How can I help you, son?"

Shaking his head, he says, "I don't know if anyone can.
How much do you know?"

I signal the waitress and ask for a couple of beers. "I'll

185

show you mine if you show me yours." Now where did I hear that lately?

He grins, but it quickly fades. Running a hand through his wiry hair, then rubbing the back of his neck, he stares at the table. When he looks up, I know we're in business.

"Max, I need help. The cops wouldn't begin to understand. I hope you can."

"I'll do my best. I'm no computer whiz, but I've got good help."

"And you know some FBI higher-ups?"

"A few."

"Maybe it'll work. But you go first, lawman."

At this point, I don't have much choice. I can sense that he probably knows something I need to help me unravel this gigantic knot. Without his help, I'm just running in place. So I tell him what I know. Except for the part about Marisol. If he's going to turn on me, I don't want her hurt.

By the time we've finished a couple of beers and I'm done talking, he's even paler than when I sat down.

"So their threats are real," he says.

"What threats?"

He regards his knuckles a moment, then takes a deep breath. "I've been getting messages the past few days. On my E-mail. Also on a CD someone sent by UPS."

"What'd they say?"

"The first one was general, something about 'evil poisons the whole system.' The next one said, 'In this world there is always danger.' "

"Ah, I recognize that one. George Bernard Shaw. But they left out a part: it ends 'for those who are afraid of it.' "

"Whatever. I am afraid. Actually, scared shitless. Anyway, last night there was one on my computer screen."

"Someone got in your apartment?"

186

He nods. "Looks that way."

"What'd it say?"

" 'Last warning. Cancel all Trojan horses.' "

"Let's get out of here."

He looks startled, but when I drop a twenty on the table and get up, he follows without complaint.

We emerge into the fading daylight, both scanning the parking lot for whatever. "Where are we going?" he says.

"Someplace we can see the stars," I say. "Makes me feel more centered when they're winking above me."

We pass by his apartment complex where he parks his 'Vette in a visitor slot, then jumps into my rental. I peel out of there, then take a couple of extra turns, checking for a tail. I don't spot one, so I head north on McAlister.

After a bit, we take Loop 1604 east to Highway 35, then turn north.

"Where are we going?" Tanger asks.

"I've got a friend who has a ranch between here and Austin. We'll stay there tonight, then catch a plane out of Austin tomorrow morning."

"To where?"

"Kansas."

"But why?"

"So we can cancel the Trojan horse or learn to ride it."

He slumps in his seat, looking out the window. "Kidnapping me won't help any."

"What?" I pull into the far right lane and cruise, wondering what he's thinking.

"When Kyle Mossler came up with the idea of embedding Trojan horses in our Securegard program, I didn't think it could be done without being detected, so I sort of ignored it as being big talk. Then we developed an algorithm and some encryption techniques to mask them. I still didn't think it was a smart idea, but I never thought he'd actually use them, or that anyone would figure out they were there, so I ignored the danger."

"So who could have found them? And why would they kill members of Zipdata?"

"I don't know, man. I just helped with the encryption. That's my thing."

"Do you know how to operate the Trojans?"

He hesitates. "So you do." I hit my brake, slowing.

He gives a half shrug. "I know the mechanics. You know, of course, that when we sold Securegard to the corporations and government agencies, we gave them total control."

"All part of the security package?"

"That's right. But with the Trojan horses in there . . . we can still gain access by transmitting the proper code."

"So you can get into the system and control the program?"

"Basically."

"Jesus."

"I thought Kyle was just phreaking. You know, just doing it to see if he could. Sort of like hacking, but in reverse. Mostly a mind game."

"David and Pete Sanders weren't in on it?"

"No. And neither were Wade or Damian."

So maybe Damian Roberts's death *was* accidental. "But how would someone know which of you could control the package?"

"From the guidebook we furnished them. We each wrote parts of it. And we gave our names in case they had specific questions as to different parts of the program."

"Then they at least know you were part of the encryption team. And they might think you could use the Trojans to compromise the system?"

He grimaces, then nods. "They *could* think that."

"If I thought of it, they did. You'd better stay with me until we can sort this out."

"How do you know we'll be safe?"

"It's not far to the ranch. You've heard of 'meanwhile, back at—' "

"Yes, sir, I know it."

"We're going to be close working pals here soon, so just call me Max."

Chapter 25

My Texas friends are glad to see me, and they welcome Will. Bob's a stockbroker who grew up in Texas—an avid fan of the Cowboys, golf, and beer—with the big-chested, brassy-skinned, round-bellied physique that often accompanies such pursuits. He hands out ice-cold Coronas all around and revs up his repertoire of gut-busting jokes, told so well that you can't help but laugh even if you've heard them before. Marjorie is a sweet-faced woman who bustles about working, but manages to keep up with the conversation and add some clever asides.

For several hours we sit in the rustic living room—catching up on our life stories, and enjoying the companionship of old friends, in spite of my brain still working on the case the whole time. Will mostly stays quiet, not knowing the couple. He seems nervous and unsettled, but there's no surprise there.

Come morning, after a solid night's sleep, we gather in the kitchen where Marjorie quickly creates wonderful smells with her great cooking skills. We all sit down to a big country breakfast of biscuits and gravy, fried eggs, bacon, spicy patty sausages, and lots of milk, orange juice, and piping hot coffee. It's easy to see where Bob got his ample paunch.

Now rested and refueled, I'm ready to roll.

"In the future, don't be such a stranger, Max," says Bob, standing on the big front porch.

"And try to stay longer next time," adds Marjorie.

"That's a deal. Sorry for the inconvenience." I can tell they know something's going on, but when I didn't volunteer any information, they didn't ask. It's nice to have savvy friends.

"You take care of yourself, buddy," Bob yells as we start to get into the car. "And call to let us know you got back to Kansas."

I smile and wave, and we hit the road, another lemming in the busy freeway herd, headed for Austin and our flight to Kansas City. Last night I called Marisol, and she said she wasn't making much progress. I told her help was on the way, and maybe we could crack this nut by tomorrow.

"I hope you're not building me up for another disappointment, Max."

"I didn't know I ever did that."

"You men."

What? But she hangs up. I hate sexist remarks.

"Do you have police protection there in Hillsboro?" says Will.

I give him a blank stare. "Oh, yeah. We do, in a loose way."

"What's that—"

"Hey, we're almost to the airport, Will. Help me watch for the rental lot to drop off this mean machine."

The rental drop-off and flight check-in both go smoothly. The plane takes off only ten minutes late. And the flight goes well, with only minor turbulence just outside Dallas that bumps us around a bit. I'm wondering if the boys tailed me to San Antonio, and if so, where they might be now. Maybe they're just watching my Trailblazer at KCI. Or maybe they booby-trapped it.

We exit the airport terminal in Kansas City, take the blue bus to satellite parking, and I manage to find my truck.

"Hold on a second," I say to Will.

There's a light coat of dust over the vehicle, and I walk around it, looking for handprints or brushed-off spots. I see nothing. Doors are all locked. I check the hood, which is closed and locked. Dropping to my knees, I peer underneath, spotting nothing unusual. Then I step back from the truck and hit the electronic door button. The lock plungers thunk upwards.

I step up and open the driver's side door and check under the seat, under the front panel, and around the ignition, seeing nothing. Then I pop the hood, open it, and stare at the motor with a grave, thoughtful expression.

"Something wrong?" Will says behind my shoulder, and I jump.

"Just making sure no vandals stole anything."

He gives me an odd look. We get in. I shut my eyes and crank the motor, which starts with a reassuring roar.

Slipping it in gear, I drive toward the exit, happy to be able to pay the parking fee.

Once on the highway, on the familiar trek between Kansas City and Hillsboro, I start to draw Will out about the Trojans and how they work. He repeats how they can be used to manipulate the system, then he adds that he thinks that the Trojans that Kyle implanted could contain viruses or worms or other self-replicating Trojans.

"So their whole computer system could become infected, and they might not be able to get it clean?"

"It would take them a long, long time to ever be sure they got it all."

"Good grief."

Then I ask about what the Securegard system was supposed to do, and how it could be sabotaged or manipulated by using the implanted back doors. He gives me a description of several scenarios, but it all starts to sound like white noise after a while. I can only process so much of what he's telling me in his alien computer jargon.

My binder with the recorder is in back, covered with the packing blanket. I don't spot any tail, so I'm breathing a little easier now. I'm thinking that maybe, with Will's and Marisol's help, we can get this case under control, just as scientists might figure out a way to detect killer asteroids and destroy them before they wipe us out.

It's all up in the air right now.

"They're on the move, Phil."

"I see that."

"Want me to follow them?"

"Let's go."

"What was the word from San Antone?" Carl asks.

"Perkins said Austin did exactly what we wanted."

"So we're good to go?"

"Yes, Carl. Stay with them."

"Hell, I'm on it."

Another trip to Wal-Mart. My plastic money must be about tapped out. Don't know if I can claim all this as expenses, or not. But people have to wear clothes, and I keep snatching them away from their normal existence. Hopefully, we can all go back to our regular lives soon.

I'm unsure whether to call Bagley. Maybe tomorrow. First, I'll let Will and Marisol jam a bit on the computer to see what they can come up with.

I drive to my house, spot no vehicles in the vicinity, and turn into the drive. Binga frolics about, glad to see me. I pet her and give her some fresh water.

"Nice place you got here," says Will. "Heck of a view."

"You can see about ten miles to the north," I say.

"Impressive."

"It's a lot prettier during the other seasons."

"This where we'll be staying?"

"No, we've got another short drive to make."

"Where to now?"

"The Flint Hills. To another ranch. A real cattle ranch this time."

"Yippee." But he's not enthusiastic.

"You don't like cows?"

"Sure, medium rare."

I go inside and check my phone messages. Amy Harrington wants me to call. Also, Lieutenant Bartles from Denver. And Jeff Bagley.

I'll call them from the ranch. I grab Binga's bowl and three cans of dog food. Then I locate my two .357 revolvers, stuffing one in the back of my pants beneath my belt, and one in front.

Outside, I whistle for Binga. She staggers up from her prone position on the porch and lurches toward us. "Get in, girl. We're going for a ride."

Once we're all settled, I give a theatrical exclamation, "Let's move out!" Both Will and Binga stare at me curiously.

I fire up the beast, then glance at Will. "Do you know how to fire a handgun?"

"I've shot a .22 rifle before. And a .38 revolver a few times. Why?"

"Just wondered. Sometimes there's snakes at the ranch."

"*Snakes?*" His eyes widen.

Why didn't I say gophers? "Just grass snakes. We shoot at them to scare them away from spooking the cows."

"The shooting doesn't make the cows stampede?"

"Not usually. Unless they're nervous. Or bored."

He gives me a strange look, but says nothing.

I drop the Trailblazer in gear and take off. Head 'em up, move 'em out. Rawhide.

An hour later, with each of us carrying a sack of groceries and a six-pack of beer, Will and I approach the basement door of the ranch house.

Marisol peeks out the door, saying, "Max, I've been wondering where you were."

"I decided to bring Binga. She'll enjoy running around in the wide open spaces. Plus, she's good at warning about strangers."

She leans down to ruffle Binga's coat and rub her head. Then she looks expectantly at Will, who's standing stiffly in the doorway.

"This's Will Tanger," I say. "He'll give us a hand in deciphering Securegard. Will, meet Marisol, a computer maven nonpareil."

"Glad to have the help," she says, extending her hand. "How are you, Will?"

"Uh, fine, thanks," he says, blushing almost as red as his hair. I'd forgotten the effect Marisol can have on men.

"I've been busy, Max. Want to hear about it?" She glances at Will as if to ask me whether to talk in front of him.

"Let's pop a top," I offer, "and we'll have a chat. It's time we started putting our heads together on this puzzle."

Chapter 26

Marisol has some stellar news. More info came in from her pal in D.C. about Carl Crabtree. He worked at the National Security Agency for fifteen years, then a year ago switched to the Department of Containment.

"That place again," I say, looking up at Marisol.

"Muy interesante," she murmurs. "But John still found *nada* on any governmental agency listings about that department."

"Did he check the address?" I ask.

"It's not legit. For that department, anyway."

"So it's a phantom agency?"

"There's a small Chinese restaurant there. John says the place was so dirty he only drank tea, even though he was starving. But it looks like a true eggroll dive."

"What do you make of all that?" I ask.

She glances at Will again. This is inside stuff, and she's probably uneasy talking about it in front of a civilian. Waggling her hand, she says, "There are some agencies that don't get mentioned to the public, as you know. John's going to ask around in case it's a front."

"But you're thinking if he asks the wrong person, we tip our hand?"

"Exacto." She sighs. "Maybe I can find out more through computer traces than by having someone nosing around in unknown territory. Especially with Will's help."

He shrugs. "I'll do what I can."

I'm very curious. "Will, how did you guys learn about this Department of Containment? How did you know they'd want your Securegard program?"

He fiddles with his hands, then pushes up his glasses. "Now that you mention it, that was odd. Pete said he got an E-mail from them. They seemed to know a lot about the program and said they were real interested in getting it."

"Out of the blue?"

"We'd sold it to NSA not long before, so we assumed they'd heard about it from them."

"So you just made the deal?"

"Right away. It didn't take long, unlike most negotiations with government agencies. And they paid with a cashier's check. We thought they were pretty cool."

"Yeah," I say absently, "way cool, around minus one hundred degrees Fahrenheit."

"Huh?" Will says.

"Como?" says Marisol.

"Oh, sorry, just musing. That's about the temperature at which dry ice sublimates. Turns from a solid to a gas."

"When do you want to go in?" Carl asks.

Phil palms his face, watching the lit-up ranch house as Carl drives past. "Give them some time. I want to see how much they know. See if maybe they passed anything on to anyone else."

"And then?"

"Probably late tomorrow morning or early afternoon. Let's go get some sleep."

Carl turns the car around to head back to Hillsboro.

Phil reaches into his briefcase, extracting a palm-sized device.

197

As they drive away, night settles over the Hill country, bringing a hard, clear sky bursting with brilliant pinpoints of light, and showing a creamy swath of stars in the Milky Way Galaxy.

Marisol and Will have been at work with the computer for the past two hours. I'm reading the latest *Scientific American* magazine, which does a good job of explaining the latest theories about the Cosmos for the lay (or in my case, lame) brain.

Occasionally the computer mavens remember I'm here and call me over to try to update me on what they've accomplished. When they try to explain how they did it, my mind turns to the gas and dust from which our Universe was created. It's all smoke and mirrors to me. But it's good there are a couple of strong techie minds on our side in this battle. God bless geeks everywhere, large and small.

At midnight, with the sound of clacking keys driving me bonkers, I say, "Hey, how about we turn in? We can always defeat the criminal universe tomorrow."

Marisol gives me a look. But I can tell from the way Will's shoulders droop that he suddenly realizes how tired he is. Marisol catches it, too, and says, "Good idea, Max."

"You guys come up with anything on the Department of Containment?"

They both frown. Will gets up and stumbles over to the couch, shaking his head. Marisol sighs, then says, "That's a tough nut to crack. All we know so far is that they like to keep a very low profile. An off-the-radar type operation, *tu sabes?*"

"Sure, I know. That's the problem. But maybe we can run a reverse Trojan horse maneuver on them."

"How's that?" Will asks, rubbing his palms on the knees of his pants.

Marisol cocks her gorgeous head, listening intently.

"We'll throw them some bait. Get them to come to us. Then spring a trap on them and find out what's going on."

"What makes you think they'll tell us?" says Marisol.

"Have you looked outside and seen the chute for castrating the boy cows?"

"You mean the bulls?"

"Sure, before. Afterwards, we call them steers."

"*Compadre,* you have a mean streak."

"Only when I'm dealing with lowlifes who murder young men. And try to ventilate my body. Brings out my penchant for revenge."

"*Soy de acuerdo.* I'm with you there."

We take turns using the bathroom, throw on some sleeping outfits, and Marisol and I retire to separate bedrooms. Binga settles in on a blanket in front of the door. Will plops down with a pillow on the living room couch.

I lie awake awhile, listening to the outdoor sounds. There's measured hooting of a couple of owls in a tree nearby. Occasional lowing by the cattle. The clickety-clackety sound of a loaded freight train, likely hauling coal to the nearby Jeffrey Energy Center. But I hear no scrunch of footsteps on the gravel drive, no snap of twigs, no screens being pulled loose. Soon, I hear nothing but the slowing cadence of my breathing.

My eyes pop open early, and I pull on my boots and slip outside to smell the morning air and the manure dropped by the cows and horses. Binga trails behind me, sniffing the ground. The horse pens sit a hundred yards away, close enough that you can't avoid the pungent odors, unless there's a favorable breeze. But the "breezes" in this part of Kansas are often roaring straight line winds or tornadoes that will lift your house off its foundation and toss it at your neighbor's barn.

Five quarter horses, all geldings, are ripping mouthfuls of hay from a thousand-pound bale in a feeder, snorting as they chomp on it, and stomping their feet. The ranch hands have picked other mounts for the day, and these steeds are missing the action. Maybe we can give them a workout later. Sitting inside watching figures on a computer screen makes me restless, too. Like them, I'd rather be out galloping across the pasture.

There's a nip in the air, it's probably around freezing, and I didn't throw on my jacket, so I inhale one last breath and turn back toward the house, glancing out toward the road as I do. A red pickup I recognize from a hog farm a few miles down the road zips by on the blacktop, followed at a distance by a shiny white Chevy Caprice. I wave at the pickup, and the man waves back. The two men in the Caprice look away as they pass. I shrug, then head back inside.

"Buenos dias, amigo," says a sleepy-eyed, tousle-haired, but still beautiful Marisol, clutching the top of her shirt together as she heads for the bathroom.

"Como amanaciste?" I ask.

"Muy bien," she says. "And you look chipper this morning."

"Just out greeting the locals. That's the horses and the farmers."

"And are they as friendly as folklore would have us city folk believe?"

"Pretty much," I say, reflecting on the stuck-up guys in the Chevy.

"What's for breakfast?" she asks.

Guess I have KP this morning. "Eggs and bacon, juice, coffee, milk. Toast, if you want."

"It all sounds good to me, *cunado*." She bats her eyes and ducks into the bathroom. Her curvy bottom leaves a fine last impression.

I turn toward the kitchen. As I pull the package of bacon from the fridge, I check to see if it came from down the road. Yep. And the eggs are from a farm not far away. I lay the carton on the counter. So what did the guys in the spotless Chevy provide?

Then a cold feeling, much more chilling than the outside air, presses around me. White, shiny car in the country where everyone has to navigate some dirt (and often muddy) roads. Two guys in the front. No ball caps or Stetsons in sight. Unfriendly, and possibly avoiding me.

Not right for this area. But how could they—

"Mornin'," says Will behind me.

I almost throw an egg against the wall. Jumpy? Not much. "Hey, Will, how'd you sleep?"

"Pretty good after I got used to the oppressive silence out here."

"Yeah, I can't sleep in the city anymore. Depends on what you're used to, I suppose."

"What're you making?"

"Eggs, any style. Bacon, crisp. Toast light or dark, your choice."

"Could I get scrambled? Light toast. Got any coffee?"

I grab a jar from the cabinet. "Here's some instant. Could you grab a pan and heat some water for me?"

"Coming up. Man, I'm starved."

"Fresh air does that for you."

"Yeah, and being kidnapped."

"I thought you came along voluntarily."

"I suppose. But I can't put up with much more of this bucolic existence. Besides, I got to get back to salvage what's left of our company."

Breaking eggs into a bowl with one hand, I say, "I understand, but you know it's not safe for you to go back until we stop these killers."

"Maybe they already got what they want."

"But I wouldn't want to take that chance, if I were you."

"Yeah, maybe not. When will those eggs be ready?"

I'm adding milk and whipping them vigorously with a fork. Then I spoon some butter into a warm skillet. "Throw some bread in that toaster, and give me five minutes."

Marisol joins us as we place the food on the table. "You know," she says, "I like living like this." That's a line from a funny country song, but I'm not sure she knows that.

"We're only here to serve and look cute," I say.

"Good thing you can cook."

Will's staring at us, wondering, I'm sure, why two older folks are acting so silly. Don't know that I could tell him. Marisol just brings out my giddy side.

We discuss the progress we've made in the case and what else needs to be done.

"Do you really have an idea how to attract the Department of Containment?" Marisol asks me.

I shoot a glance at Will. "If Will doesn't mind me dangling him as bait."

"Like how?" he says.

"We'll let them know you're willing to cooperate, give them the info they want about the Trojans, and indicate that you'll dissolve the company, if necessary."

"You really think they'll buy that?"

"I think they'll have to feel us out on the offer."

"Hmmm. I don't know. Maybe it would—"

"Wait a minute," Marisol says. "Won't we tip them off about what we know?"

"Not if we're careful what we say."

We each reflect on the idea as we finish breakfast. The cold orange juice tastes crisp and fresh and very juicy.

Country air seems to sharpen the taste buds.

Marisol relents her position of woman of leisure by gathering the dirty dishes and placing them in the sink. I can tell she briefly searches for a dishwasher that doesn't exist. "You wash, I'll dry," I say.

She frowns, but runs some water into the sink and splashes in some dish soap. "They can soak while we gear up our plan."

"Let's go," I say, and we all find places around the computer, with Marisol at the keyboard.

This should be a real challenge.

Chapter 27

The plan has been set in motion. We sent a message to the Department of Containment suggesting that Will wanted to meet to work out a peaceful agreement. Marisol composed the note, hinting that Will might be willing to discuss the security breaches and to dissolve the Zipdata company, now that key members were gone.

We sent my cell phone number as a contact point, and now we're waiting for a call. But I want to have a workable plan, so I'm outside, reconnoitering the area. Although I'm familiar with the lay of the land here, I want to visualize whatever advantages I may use against the city boys they're sure to send.

The horses might be a plus, and I ask Will and Marisol to come with me to saddle them up. In the pen, both Will and Marisol are very wary of where they step. They're probably afraid a little manure might disintegrate their fine footwear. The horses paw the ground and snort big clouds of vapor, uneasy as the strange group of humans gathers close. I'm patting the flank of a quarter horse, trying to get him to settle, and taking in the sharp leathery smell of horsehide and sweat.

Marisol has done this before, and she's doing pretty well at it. Will is fumbling with the leather, as jumpy as a skittish colt, and he might spook the horse and get kicked. I hope I don't lose my patience and kick him myself.

"That's good, Will," I say. "Now wait until he breathes

out, then tighten the girth cinch. That way, the saddle won't do a flip and leave you upside-down."

His brow is furrowed, but he watches Slowpoke until his chest deflates, and then pulls the leather cinch tighter, slipping the tongue of the buckle into another hole.

"Excellent, cowpoke. Now stick the end of the strap behind the tightened part, pull the stirrup off the saddle horn and let it dangle, and I'll show you how to give him the bit."

"Can't you just do it for me?" Will says. His eyes are wide and pleading. And he's pale.

"Sure I can, Will. And maybe I'll fall off my horse in the pasture and break my leg. Then, when you're all alone out there, you can ask the bad guys to give you a hand."

He frowns, but nods in submission. "So how do you do it?"

I take off the horse's halter, loop it around his neck, and cinch it.

"Now look," I say, taking the bridle and bit in my left hand, the reins in my right, "you just need to slip it in his mouth until it settles in behind his teeth. Be gentle, but firm, and he'll let you do it. Here, hold it like this."

Will approximates the position. Starts to insert the bit. "He's got his lips closed," he whines.

"Sure, he's seen this act before. Here, just push the bit against his lips until he starts to part them, then push it straight back into his mouth. Stick your fingers in there a little if you have to. Pry those jaws apart."

"Oh, God," he says, but does it, and Slowpoke gives up and accepts the metal rod inside his mouth with a shiver of protest.

"Great, now just slip the bridle over his head, stick that looped part around one ear, and wrap the reins around the saddle horn."

After much wrestling, adjusting, and gnashing of his teeth and the horse's, he gets it done.

"Man, you've just made Cowboy, Grade One," I say.

He gives me a huge smile. Then Slowpoke jerks his head around and bumps him, whinnying a challenge.

"When he starts that stuff, grab the opposite rein and give it a jerk."

Slowpoke gives me the evil horse eye.

"So let's ride," I say.

And after a few minutes' instructions on technique, Marisol, then Will, then I mount up and head uncertainly but boldly out of the pen and into the pasture.

The Sun is rising higher in the sky behind us, casting our shadows before us, air nippy but bracing, and the horses soon warm to the idea of going out for a pasture adventure. We start by walking them a bit, then work up to a trot. Marisol looks pretty comfortable as her butt rises and falls back onto the saddle, but Will looks like a marionette being jerked up and down by his puppeteer. He'll be stiff and sore tomorrow.

Just in case it's needed, I get them to lope the horses, which is actually a much smoother gait, making you feel like you're gliding across the pasture, just one with the horse, building incredible speed. Of course, you pray the big critter doesn't step into a gopher hole or trip over a rock, sending himself and you ass over teakettle.

Those maneuvers learned, we slow back to a walk, and I begin to scope out various places for their strategic value. Ahead, there's a grove of walnut trees, and a little stream winds through there. Nice place to stop for some shade and water. Also, a fine place to set up a few tricks to put city gangsters off balance.

The operative, a tall, muscular man named Bill, strides

down the hall, knocks on a closed door, then enters. He hands his boss the message from Kansas, waits until the man behind the large desk has read it, then asks him, "What should we do, John?"

From his leather chair, John smiles, but it's a sad, plaintive expression. "I suppose we'd better send our men for a meet. I think it's come down to this, don't you agree?"

Operation Secure Stop has been Bill's to run for the past several months, and he's been in hot water over the recent situation. He'd love to see it go away.

"I think that's best," he agrees.

"Then make the call."

"Get that," says Bones.

Carl grabs up the cell phone and says hello, listens, then hands the receiver to Bones.

"Yes?" Several seconds go by. "Okay, I understand. But do you think we should agree to meet them there? Oh . . . well, all right. We'll do it and call you later."

"What's up?" Carl says as Bones hangs up.

"Looks like it's showtime," he says. "Let's trade this Caprice for a van, stop by a gun store, and then we'll head back to the ranch."

We leave the horses in the corral slurping water from a circular trough, but still liveried up and ready to ride. I also saddle up two other horses, walk them over to the ranch house, and tie them to a pipe railing. Then we grab a snack. We've just finished, when my cell phone sounds off with a Mozart riff. Everyone freezes as though they'd been electrocuted. After a couple more rings, I hit the button and say hello.

"Is this Austin?"

"That's right, partner."

"Don't start that cowpoke shit with me. We'll meet you there because we were ordered to. But if you try anything fancy, you'll be sorry."

"I'm sure. How far away are you?"

"We'll be there in an hour."

"Come to the lower level of the ranch house." And I hang up.

Everyone, including Binga, who has wandered over for attention, stares at me as though I've suddenly grown another head. To break the tension, I reach into my pocket and fish out a biscuit. "Here, girl, let's see you do Circus Dog."

She cocks her head, then when I hold up the biscuit, the circuits fire in her furry head, and she crouches down, ready to pounce. She still has good eye-to-mouth coordination, not having missed a tossed treat for at least a year. I let it fly, and she lunges, baring her fangs. Ever the crowd-pleaser, she nabs the morsel with a loud chomp, then pins it to the ground beneath her paws and sets to gnawing in earnest. Applause breaks out all around.

"All right, ladies and gents, the show's over. Now it's time for the main event. We've got less than an hour; here's what I want you to do."

"What do you think, Bones?"

"Drive up within thirty yards, stop, and we'll get out. If they don't show their faces right away, I'll call Austin on his cell. We'll disarm them, find out about the Trojan horses in the program, then disable the damn things."

"Then we'll disable *them*," Carl says, grinning.

"That's the best part. I'm ready to get the hell out of Kansas."

We're approaching the shady watering hole. The horses

weren't that happy to return to the pasture, thinking, I imagine, that they'd be feted with hay and grain for the remainder of the day. I figure they're being paid from nine to five, so they can still put in some honest labor for a while longer.

"Do you think they'll come out here, Max?" asks Marisol.

"If they want Will to help them."

"What if they see it as a better opportunity to kill us?"

"I imagine those odds are constant. Sort of like a comet's orbit. After you chart it for a while, you know where it's going, and when it'll be back."

Will doesn't look like a happy horse rider. His steed looks pissy, too. Can't we all just get along?

Binga trots ahead and makes for the stream. She slurps up a goodly amount, then flops down on her side. Her eyes close, sides heave, and her tongue sticks out between her teeth— she's already out.

"Let's dismount," I say, sounding like the crusty sergeant in a bad cavalry flick.

We climb down from our noble mounts and tie them off to some low limbs. I take a brief mental inventory of our supply of arms. I'm carrying my .357 Smith & Wesson revolver, the big one, and Marisol has her Glock, a 10mm job. Then I remember something, and I catch her eye.

"Marisol, do you still carry that derringer?"

She looks sheepish. Not good in cattle country. "*Si, eso es.* It's still against regulations, and I still do it." She pulls up a pants leg, showing her calf with a holster strapped tight on the shapely muscle, the flat S&W .22-caliber derringer snugged into it.

"That's beautiful," I say.

She gives me a look.

"Both cosmetically and concealment-wise."

Her face opens like a desert blossom, thoughts flitting behind those almond-shaped eyes with their deep coffee color. Then she moves close, peers into my soul, and leans forward, her warm cheek nuzzling against my neck and cheek, pressing her body against mine. "Max, I've been recalling a lot of memories these past couple of days. I'm not sure we should have let our relationship slip away when I moved."

She feels perfect, smells great, raises my blood pressure a good thirty points. "I've had the same thoughts, Marisol. But I didn't want to bring them up. You know I still have feelings for you, but I couldn't take the long-distance romance. Particularly when you seemed more interested in moving up in the Bureau than in building our relationship."

"I've finally become aware that some things are more important than the Job." She moves back, taking me in with her eyes.

Thoughts of the past flicker in my mind's eye. With strong regrets, I decided to move on after she had gone to Miami and I was still in Puerto Rico. Then when my potential transfer to Florida turned into one to Texas, it really quashed any possibility of making it work.

"Marisol, I can't say I haven't thought of you over the years."

"I have, too, Max. Even after you got married."

And I was happy with Sharon. But now she's gone. "So, you're still in D.C., and I'm here in faraway Kansas."

"Hey, guys," Will says, "those thugs could be here soon."

I turn my head. He looks agitated, his forehead moist. I'll bet his hands are as wet and clammy as a codfish. "You're right, Will. Let's get our act together."

I turn back to Marisol, squeeze her arms, then pull her to me for a brief, but very satisfying kiss.

"So, *caballeros*," I say, "let's prepare to muzzle those mongrel dogs."

Binga raises her head and gives me a curious stare.

"I just meant some bad guys, girl. Nothing to worry about."

I study the setup again, as if it's the scenery for a stage play. Which, in a way, it is. I go over the details: I've stuck a small .357 revolver in the crook of a nearby tree. Put a couple of throwing knives beneath the edge of a large rock. Strapped a knife to my lower leg, hid a leather-bound sap in a bush, got my knife belt buckle snugged in place.

I hand Will a leather slapper, meant for making a loud sound when you smack it against a horse's flank. The huge beasts are very attuned to noise, you get their attention immediately, and they react at once. Will sticks it in his back pocket and listens to my instructions.

". . . when I say the word 'thunder,' okay, Will?"

"I'll try, Max. Anyway, you guys know what you're doing with those guns, right? You're supposed to protect me. I'm valuable to you, remember?"

Marisol rolls her eyes, but I give the lad a reassuring smile and a pat on the arm. "Sure, Will, we're highly trained. Nothing to worry about."

"Those guys seem to be trained, too," he says.

"But we have nature on our side."

Both of them give me a look. But I know what I'm talking about. I hope.

"Let's stand over here," I say, motioning them to follow.

"What's the plan, Max?" asks Marisol.

"Nothing too fancy," I say. "I hope we can just talk our way into a solution. Surely these guys won't want to cause a bloodbath out here."

She looks doubtful. "I don't think we know what they'll do."

"That's why we'll use every advantage. You ever watch Westerns?"

Her pretty brow crinkles. "Sometimes."

Will's expression opens like a sunflower. "You're talking about using the Sun as an advantage in a gunfight."

"Very good, Will. This time of year, especially, when it's low in the sky, we want it at our backs and in their eyes. Makes a big difference."

"Some hand grenades wouldn't hurt," says Marisol.

"We'd be too close. Explosives don't pick favorites."

"So we debate, duck, and maybe duel?" she says.

"That's about all I've got." I shrug. Doesn't sound like much when she says it. But I still believe in the power of the natural world. And I hope I'm more attuned to it than the goons are.

"Who's that?" says Carl as they approach the turn-in to the ranch.

A battered white pickup pulls out of the entrance and turns in the opposite direction. Bones watches them through the binocs.

"Looks like a couple of ranch hands."

"Good. Fewer witnesses."

"Hope there's no more out there." He scans the pastures, seeing nothing but cattle and snow and some trees.

Carl motions to the backseat. "You bringing the Mini-14?"

Bones gives a stingy grin, nodding. "You bet. And some sleeping potion," he adds, nudging the cooler with his foot.

Carl drives the van up to the ranch house. They scan the area, seeing nothing. No one's outside. Except a couple of horses. Laughing to himself, Carl says, "Think they got up a posse?"

Chapter 28

Bones calls out several times to the ranch house. But it remains as silent as a fence post on the prairie. Carl tries—louder and more insistent. The nearby horses stamp their feet and snort. There's still no response.

"Let's try the cell," Bones says. He calls the number, watches for any movement. Then he hears a click.

"Max speaking."

"We're here for the meeting. Come on out."

"Can you see the door?"

"Yeah, why?"

"The *note* on it?"

Bones spots the folded sheet of paper stuck in the storm door. *What the hell is this? Some kind of trick?*

"Why don't you come out," he says, "and tell us what's on your mind?"

"We're not there. We took a little ride while we were waiting. Come join us, it's a nice afternoon."

Bones covers the phone with his hand and gestures toward the door. "Go get that stupid piece of paper."

Carl glances at it, looking wary. Bones lets out an irritated huff, rips open the van's door and yanks out the Mini-14. "If anyone blinks, I'll blow their head off."

Carl frowns, but makes his way in a zigzag pattern toward the house, moving alongside the horses, using them for cover, then trots the last ten feet to the door, grabs the note, and retreats like a scared deer. Behind the car, he opens it and they read: MOUNT UP, GUYS. WE'RE IN THE PASTURE TO THE WEST. (THAT'S TOWARD THE WINDMILL.) JUST FOLLOW THE COW PATH AND YOU'LL SEE US BY THE GROUP OF WALNUT TREES.

"What's a walnut tree look like?" asks Carl.

"Just get on the fuckin' horse."

"I only been on one of those things twice in my life," Carl whines. "What if it tries to buck me off?" His eyes look glazed.

"Hang on to the reins, and watch what I do," says Bones. "These plugs will do good to walk there without going lame." He unties the reins of the chestnut gelding, sticks his foot in the stirrup, and swings himself aboard. "And, I swear, Carl, those pricks are going to pay for this little game."

"Here they come," says Marisol.

Damn, she's got good eyes. "Okay, spread apart. And everyone relax. This will go as smooth as Cool Whip."

They ride up, not in a cloud of dust as in the movies, but looking like a ragtag, stringy tumbleweed covered with shaggy horsehair. Bones is in front, looking comfortable in the saddle. Carl has his elbows out as he death grips the reins, his face pinched and white around the mouth, squinting against the sun. Bones has a Ruger rifle across his lap, looking confident with it. Carl probably couldn't get to his gun without falling off his mount.

They stop a short distance away.

"Come on down, guys," I say. "We won't bite."

Bones eases off his horse, keeping control of the short rifle all the way. Carl dismounts, unsure what to do with the horse now that he's off it. Bones finds a low branch and ties the reins to it. Carl tries to do the same, not getting the leather straps secured. They face us, not looking like happy cowpokes.

Bones raises the muzzle of his Mini-14. Damn, that thing looks menacing. "Let's get rid of your hardware."

"Can't do it, Bones," I say. "We have to talk first."

He studies me for a moment. Then he angles the muzzle toward Will. "How about you, son? You packing?"

Will looks ready to faint. I think he's quit breathing. But he squeezes out, "No . . . no, sir. I don't have anything."

Bones glances back at me, shading his eyes from the sun. "Then, assuming the others do, I'm sure they won't want you to get shot before they give them up."

Damn. Our Achilles heel. He found it right off.

"Listen, Max," Bones says in a reasonable voice, "we're not going to hurt anyone. We'll just feel better if you're not holding any heat. Then we can talk business."

The horses sense the tension. Our mounts are pawing at the ground. The horse Bones rode here is angling away from him. The bay that Carl tied up poorly yanks his head a couple of times, loosening the straps. They still hold him, but maybe if he got spooked, he'd be able to . . .

And now a low growl catches everyone's attention. Binga. I look at her, seeing the hair on her back bristling, her tail going down, head held low.

Carl pulls his pistol, frightened.

"No, Binga. That's all right, girl. Sit," I say.

She hesitates, gives Bones and Carl another death ray stare, then settles uneasily in the snow, her haunches still tense, ready to pounce if needed.

"Good girl," I say, dipping my hand into my jeans pocket, grabbing a biscuit.

"Hold it," says Bones, swinging the cannon in my direction.

"Just a biscuit," I say, holding it out, then shoving it in my shirt pocket. "No weapons, honest."

"Okay, everyone cut the bullshit." He pulls a pillowcase from inside his coat and throws it on the ground at my feet. "Put your guns, or whatever you have, in there now, or Will gets it, then the rest of you. Max, you'll get to see your pretty girlfriend die in agony before I pop you."

I'm wondering where in the hell he got the pillowcase. Is that standard issue for hitmen? Anyway, this situation sucks, and I can't see it getting better anytime soon. Hope my backup plans work better than my main one. Hey, couldn't be any worse.

"All right, Bones. Ease off. You can have our guns. We just want to talk, anyway. We don't intend to hurt you."

"No worries there. Let's see the metal, use two fingers, do it slow."

I pull my revolver from its holster, thumb and forefinger holding the grips, then slip it into the pillowcase.

After long seconds of held breaths, pounding hearts, and tense trigger fingers, our guns are in the bag. Except for Marisol's derringer. And, oops, I forgot to add the knife that's strapped to my leg.

"Let's sit down," says Bones, indicating the large fallen log lying in the small clearing. There's a couple of good-sized limestone boulders nearby. I pick the one with the throwing knives beneath it, as it looks the most comfy. Unfortunately, Carl is between me and the tree with the extra revolver. But nothing in life is perfect.

Bones seems tense. Carl looks more relaxed. He was more worried about the animals doing him harm than the humans. But he'd do well to consider all the dangers. Because the prairie can be fraught with them.

After questioning Will for ten minutes, Bones seems satisfied that the kid will be able to remove the Trojan horses implanted in the security program, and that the other kids left in the company will cooperate with whomever Bones represents.

"So, who do you represent?" I ask.

His eyes narrow. "Let's just say it's a vested interest that's not to be screwed with."

"You know," I say, "cracking is a common phenomenon. So Kyle went too far with the Trojans, but no harm was done with them. I think he just wanted to see if he could pull it off."

Carl gives a derisive snort.

Bones looks thoughtful. "Maybe that's true, but we couldn't take a chance on that. And we don't want any copycats, either."

"But now Will and David and Pete will spread the word that cracking and phreaking have become very dangerous activities," I say, "and, hopefully, the computer geeks will take heed and cease and desist their attacks. So, are we all square?" I slap my thighs and rise to my feet.

Bones stands and covers me with the rifle. I was afraid of that. Not what the Potawatomi Indians would call a good omen.

"Have you guys ever seen a Circus Dog?" I say. Binga's ears perk up. I pretend to scratch my chest, but I'm sure she can see my hand is close to that tasty biscuit.

Carl lurches to his feet. Even he senses that something's up. "What the hell are you yakking about?"

"This!" I grab the end of the biscuit and toss it in the air, close to the bothersome rifle.

Binga's adrenaline must still be pumping, because she make the grandest, most forceful leap she's pulled off in years. She brushes the gun barrel aside, and I lunge toward it, grabbing the cold steel tube to keep it pointed the other way.

Carl pulls out his .45, but as Bones and I struggle, I manage to keep the skinny guy between me and Monster Man.

With Carl distracted, I see Marisol reaching down to her lower pants leg.

But now Bones jerks hard on the rifle, and the thing explodes, shattering the quiet of the clearing. Binga yelps in pain, a loud shriek that cuts to my heart. I throw a hard overhand right into Bones's face, and a gusher of blood spurts from his nose. I yank the rifle away and fling it into the creek, then drive a low left hook into his gut that twists his face into prune-like agony. He does a slow crumple to the ground, and contracts into a fetal position, clutching his belly.

"Sounds like thunder!" I yell.

Will pulls the slapper from his back pocket and smacks it against a tree trunk, making a loud crack, like that of a .22 pistol. The nervous bay can't stand any more, and he snorts, pulls the reins free from the branch, then bucks twice and gallops off toward the barn. The second kick catches Carl squarely in the butt, sending him sprawling face first into the snow, his big .45 tumbling into the weeds. Now he looks up, spitting snow from his mouth. To his surprise, he finds Marisol with her derringer stuck in his ear.

I rip the 9mm pistol from Bones's holster, then turn to Binga, who crawls toward me dragging her bloody haunch, her eyes scared and pleading. "Easy, girl, just lie still." I hold her head and she moans and whimpers, but she doesn't struggle.

I handcuff Bones, and Marisol does the same to Carl. Then I toss her my cell phone and give her a number to call. "Tell the sheriff we're holding two prisoners in the walnut grove to the west of the ranch house." He's hunted pheasant here before and knows the place.

She looks doubtful, but she punches in the number as I get

Carl and Bones settled on the ground, their backs against the log.

Binga whines, and I lean down and check her wound. Damn, it looks bad. She's losing a lot of blood, and I'm scared she could go into shock, so I pull out my handkerchief and tie it around her leg.

As I retrieve my revolver from the crook in the tree, I motion to Will, and he comes over. "Will, I hope you were telling me straight about being able to use a handgun. I want you to take this in case Marisol has any problems. You're her backup. But don't pull it out unless there's an emergency."

He takes the gun, a frightened look on his face, sticks it in his belt and zips his coat over it. I hope I've made a wise decision. Only once before have I entrusted a civilian with a weapon. That was for him to watch my back when our federal building was being shot up and bombed by a weirdo with three handguns and a briefcase full of pipe bombs.

Now Marisol snaps the phone shut and turns to me. "Okay, Max. They're on their way."

"Marisol," I say, my gaze locking her with trust and love. "I've got to get Binga to a vet. Do you think you could hold them until the sheriff—"

She holds up a hand. "Go on, Max. I've got it under control." She retrieves her 10mm Glock and points it at Carl's oversize head. "If one of these mutts makes a wrong move, I'll blast both of them and sort it out later. It'll be my word against . . . let's see. Hey, it'll just be *my* word."

She gives the punks an evil stare, and I smile, then change my expression to stern. "I think that's the way to handle it. I'll come back as soon as I can."

"Take your time, Max. Get Binga the help she needs."

I grab Smokey's reins, lead him over to where Binga lies in a gathering pool of crimson against the glowing white snow, and ask Will to steady the wary horse. Then I lift Binga as gently as I can, and drape her over the horse's haunches. She groans, then passes out.

Tying her limp form in place as fast as I can, I then mount up, yell, "Go!" and dig my heels into the horse's flanks. We take off across the pasture in a frantic lope. No time to waste. Binga saved us all; I'm not going to let her die.

Chapter 29

Binga's lying on the front seat beside me where I can watch her. I'm glancing at her, then back to the road as I fly along it at eight-five-plus, my Trailblazer leaning into the curves, then barreling down the straightaways. The old gal is conscious now, and she's breathing okay, but she's moaning and still bleeding like crazy. And you can't tell if a German shepherd's going pale.

There's a vet I know in the nearby town of Onaga. It's four-thirty. I hope to hell he's still there.

I squeal into town, make a turn, and floor it for the last few blocks to the vet's office. My truck slides into the gravel parking lot and scrunches to a halt in front of the building. Then I hustle around to the passenger door, pull Binga out, and cradle her bloody form in my arms.

Hobbling under the weight, I make it to the door and barge inside. The receptionist, a wan teenager with bluish hair, looks up in alarm, her eyes getting big behind her granny glasses. "Can I help you?" she asks.

"She's got a gunshot wound. We need to see Dr. Allen—now!"

She takes a look at Binga, goes ashen, and points to her left. "Take her into exam room one, and I'll get Dr. Allen." She turns and rushes to the back office.

In the exam room, I lay Binga on a stainless steel table abutting a Formica-topped bench with cabinets. As I talk to her in a low voice, she whimpers in pain. The back door jumps open, and Dr. Allen charges in, his bulk filling the space, his brown eyes taking in both me and Binga.

"Hi, Max, what've we got?"

I tell him about the gunshot wound and when it happened. He pulls on some rubber gloves and pets Binga's head with soothing strokes, telling her to relax, his voice mellow and calm. He calls for his assistant, opens a package of gauze pads and holds them against the wound, then dabs at it to get a better look.

The girl comes in, and he tells her to hold the pads in place.

"How's it look, Stan?" I ask.

"Not as bad as I first thought. It's bloody, but not a critical wound."

The doc fills a syringe with liquid from a vial, pinches the flesh at Binga's ruff, and slips in the needle. As the painkiller goes in, Binga sighs and her rigid frame relaxes. Her eyes blink, then close, and her breathing slows.

After telling his assistant what instruments he needs, he starts trying to calm me down. We've known each other for ten years, and I've seen him handle lots of animals at the ranch; I know he's good. That helps me compose myself.

"It'll take a few minutes until she's totally out," he says. "I'll clean the wound and stitch it up. After that, she'll sleep overnight, so you don't have to stay here, unless you want to."

I do want to, but I'm nervous about Marisol being left alone with the bad guys. "I need to handle something urgent, then I'll come back and check on her."

I give him my cell phone number, then rub Binga behind the ears, getting no response. So I turn and ease out the door. Once outside the building, I dial the sheriff's office.

A man answers. His voice sounds familiar, and I say,

"This is Max Austin with the FBI. Actually, I'm a P.I. now."

"Hey, how are you, Max? This is Travis Wilson, the undersheriff."

"I thought I knew your voice." I ask him how he's doing, then ask, "Has the sheriff left?"

"He's in his office. Is something wrong?"

Maybe so. "Let me talk to him." He switches me over.

"Sheriff Halvorsen."

"Hank—Max Austin. Did you get a call from our ranch a while ago?"

"Nope, I been here for the past two hours, and it's been quiet. What's going on?"

Damn. That's a good question. "I can't explain it now, but could you and Travis get over to the ranch right away? I'll call you on your cell to fill you in, but I've got to head there myself."

I roar out of the parking lot; this doesn't feel right.

Turning into the entrance, I can see the van still parked beside the ranch house. I creep along the gravel road, watching for any movement inside the house or out. A man exits the lower level and approaches the van. I'm getting too close, he might spot me, so I pull off the road into the pasture, putting the house between me and him. It looked like Carl.

I kill the engine and coast. This can't be good. What is Carl doing free, walking around? Is Marisol okay . . . and Will? Did those pricks kill them, and now they're waiting for me?

The Chevy rolls to a stop, and I ease out of the door and push it closed. I've got to take the chance that no one looks out a window and sees me. I need to get close enough to see what's going on. If the sheriff comes barreling up, whatever chance Marisol and Will might have left will vanish. So, crouching low, my magnum in hand, I sneak up to the house.

"Hey, Bones, let's get moving," Carl yells.

I can only make out dark forms inside. Ducking, I slip around the far side of the house where I'll be able to see the van. As I catch my breath and peek around the corner, I see Bones and Marisol and Will all approaching the van. No one's tied up—that's very curious. So I go down on one knee, steadying myself, and listen like a rabbit.

"C'mon, man," Carl says. "He might come back."

"If he does, we'll take care of him, like we should've done before." An evil grin spreads across Bones's face.

Marisol stiffens. "Don't forget, we have a deal, guys."

Bones turns to her. He keeps smiling. Will is standing nearby, not getting involved. "Take it easy, lady. I'm just letting off some steam. I'll go along with the plan."

"Anyway, Carl's right," she says. "You'd better go."

Bones shakes his head. "That goofy boyfriend of yours is still holding the dog's paw and making a sad face. He probably gave the mutt some mouth-to-mouth on the way."

Marisol puts her hand on the butt of her Glock. Why does she still have her gun, and why are these people even talking with each other? Has the world taken a crazy, off-kilter spin while I was gone?

"If he gets back here before you leave"—she lets it hang there a moment, then continues—"all bets are off."

Bones gives her a smirk, then opens the passenger door and climbs in, while Carl starts up the van. Bones rolls down the window and says, "Now, Cassandra, don't be angry with us."

Cassandra? What's he mean calling her that?

Marisol and Will back away from the van, and Carl pulls ahead a short distance, then stops and backs up to turn around. The rear of the van is facing me. Now he begins to turn, heading the other direction, and I move fast toward the side. As the van gets even with Marisol, Carl slows, sticks his head out, and says, "Good-bye, cutie. Hope you—"

And then he sees my revolver pointing at his nose. "Freeze, meathead. You, too, Bones."

Carl slams on the brakes. The van shudders. And Bones throws open the door and scrambles out the other side.

"Damnit!" I say. And for a moment I wonder if Marisol will back me up on this play. Sure, she will. I think.

I have to take care of Carl, so I yank open the door and grab him by his coat at the shoulder, jerking him out hard. He tumbles to the ground, making a big depression in the snow. I reach down and pull his .45 from the holster. "Don't move," I say, and he seems to get the message. Then I turn to where Bones will be coming around the front of the van.

"Now don't *you* move, dumbass."

Oh, hell, Bones went around the back end, and he's got me cold. I glance at Marisol. She's got her pistol out, but she's not pointing it at Bones. In fact, it's aimed at me.

"Drop the six-gun, Austin," Bones says. "And anything else you're packing. But move real slow, or I might get nervous and twitch."

I glance around, searching, and there stand the horses, giving me an idea. Then I shoot a quick glance at Will, a question mark on my face, trying to ask if he still has the revolver and if he's on my side. But he just stares at me with a dazed, blank look on his face.

"Drop it now," says Bones. Man, he's impatient.

So I dangle my revolver from one finger, and I inch toward the nags they rode earlier. "Here." I drop the revolver into the snow and step away from it, getting closer to the geldings.

"Stand still." Bones juts his chin at my revolver. Carl retrieves it and sticks it in his belt.

"Wait a minute," I say. "Marisol, what the heck's going on?"

She looks sad. "It's a complicated story, Max." She re-grips her gun, a sure sign she's nervous.

"I doubt I'm going anywhere, so tell me."

"Forget it, Marisol," says Bones. "We got things to do."

Her eyes narrow like a snake's. "He has a right to ask. This is a big shock to him."

She's putting that mildly. I nod in agreement.

She lowers the muzzle of her pistol and stares at me thoughtfully. "Max, our country's in trouble. Crackers and virus writers have gotten more sophisticated, shrewder. They're doing more damage—causing huge financial losses, even weakening our national security."

"I know, but—"

"Just let me say it. This is hard enough."

I shrug. Carl leans against the van. Bones just glares at me, waiting.

"The FBI started out behind the curve in computer knowledge, and despite that, everyone expected us to stop cybercrime, and fast. We used consultants and hired top-rate talent, trying to keep up with the deluge of new and better crackers, but we still lost ground. Then we caught a break: one of the guys we'd arrested agreed to talk to save himself from a deuce behind bars." I stare at her, waiting for the rest.

She sighs, then goes on. "He gave us a vital guy we'd been wanting to catch but could never pin with a violation. So, when word got around about the pending arrest and potential headlines, an assistant director decided he should get in on the action. Even wanted to go on the arrest."

"Ah, I see," I comment. "The lame and halt joining in the fray of battle." Bureau brass aren't promoted because of their competence in solving cases, making arrests, or testifying in court. In short, being lousy agents, to keep out of trouble they go "the administrative route." I nod my head, saying, "And he botched it."

"Big time, Max. Unbelievable."

"What happened?"

Bones holds up a hand. "Let's cut this short. We got to move."

And he doesn't even know the posse's on the way.

Marisol cuts him a hard look, then holsters up. "You watch him," she says, "and I'll finish the story."

Bones sighs. "Hurry up."

She turns her pretty face back to me. "We cornered the guy in his garage as he was wheeling out a mower. The AD pulled his gun, the muzzle shaking all around, and his voice squeaked when he told the guy to assume the position. It was all the rest of us could do to keep from falling on the ground laughing."

"But he made the arrest?"

"Sort of. One of the other agents frisked the guy, then pulled out his cuffs. But the AD had holstered his Glock and turned his back to the perp, smiling as though he thought the cameras were rolling for his close-up. The bad guy glanced over his shoulder, saw this, then pushed off the car, grabbed the AD's pistol, and swung it all around. Everyone froze."

"C'mon," says Bones. "Finish up, and let's get moving."

One of the horses whinnies. The other one paws the ground. They can sense the tension, and it's making them nervous.

"Bottom line is, the guy figured out the AD was the big shot, so he pulled him close, held the gun to his temple, and told us all to back away from the car. We could see he planned to take the idiot for a ride. And the way the guy was acting, we weren't sure the AD would be coming back."

"So someone stopped him?"

She nods stiffly. "Yes, I had the angle. For a moment, I couldn't decide which of them more deserved to be shot. Then I took out the bad guy."

"Oh, my God, Marisol." I can see from the sag of her shoulders that it took her out, too. "I'm so sorry." Citizens don't realize that shooting someone, even a criminal, has a terrible psychological effect on a law enforcement officer. Many never recover from it.

"Then the AD couldn't own up to the real story," she continues. "Before it was over, we all had to swear to a cover-up version. He let me know that if I brought up the straight version, I'd be in big trouble over the shooting. The ungrateful prick."

"And the Bureau bought it?"

"Even the director thought it was best. He figured we'd send a message to the 'hackers,' as he called them, that their activities were a serious crime. That the FBI would stop them, no matter what it took."

"But how did it come to using these fools?"

Carl and Bones both give me a scowl.

"During the meetings about the shooting incident, someone mentioned it was a good way to take hackers out of the game for good. Funny, at first, then a few guys got serious about it. The director, seeing the great publicity if we could somehow get on top of the problem, said for them to handle the matter however they could."

"Why did you go along with it?"

"They held the shooting over my head, then said if I'd stay with the 'project' for a year, they'd make me a fast-rising star in the Bureau."

I shake my head. "In their universe of death and deception."

She can't meet my gaze. I ask, "What did you have to do?"

She hesitates, then says in a low voice, "I helped select the real problem crackers. And I sent out the assignments to the phony group we set up—the Department of Containment."

"Where'd those guys come from?"

"Misfits and malcontents from different agencies who were on the verge of getting disciplined or canned. They were given a choice to join an elite team for a secret assignment to further national security. We had five teams of two."

Bones gets a disgusted look on his face. Carl apparently lost interest, and he's looking for something in the back of the van. I'm feeling sick.

"You sent out assignments?" I say.

"I'd send photos and descriptions of the targets. Then they'd do the hits. We had members of the lab working on methods of killing that were hard to detect, thinking it had to do with covert assassinations of world crime figures and anti-American politicos."

"Then you learned that I was involved in one of the cases."

"Yes, and I couldn't believe it, but I felt I had to protect you. These guys here didn't know who I was, I'd always contact them by secure teletype and fax, using a code name. But when you took Binga to the vet, I was able to convince them of my position."

I'm trying to compute that. And I'm wondering where the sheriff is. I know his office is far away, but I'm getting a little stressed here.

Bones pulls out a photo, then turns it over. "She knew about the stamp of the woman's head on the photos. She was 'Cassandra,' the contact we got orders from."

Cloak and dagger stuff always annoys me. "Peachy. Very clever setup."

Bones and Carl seem agitated. They both come up close as

if to intimidate me with their very presence, and it's working. Carl pulls a pair of handcuffs from his back pocket.

I hear a snort and glance at the horses, seeing that they're restless, with the bay stomping his back foot, and the chestnut pawing at the snow. I move another step closer to them, saying in a theatrical voice, "What's with the cuffs?" The chestnut gelding shivers, startled.

"What do you think, dickhead?" Bones has clearly lost any sense of humor.

"Okay, no one move," says a shaky voice. All heads turn toward Will, who's standing there with my revolver in his trembling hand. I'm sure we're all wondering if the gun's about to go off, and if we're in harm's way.

Bones gets that ugly sneer on his face. "We've got three people with guns, Will. You'd better drop that before you find yourself good and dead."

He's got a point, but Will sticks to his gun. And he assumes an even tougher stance. "Then I'll take you out first, Bones."

That's a smart threat, and Bones seems to be thinking it over. Marisol hasn't made a move, and I can't see her harming Will, but then there's Carl. He's stupid and dangerous, and I decide I'd better jump him.

But it's too late. The big moron whips out a pistol, and before Will can even think about what to do, Carl pumps two shots into his chest. Will drops like a slaughtered cow.

I churn my legs as I drive into Carl, knocking him to the ground. Then I smash his face with a solid punch, but he comes up with his pistol pointed at my eye. And another handgun presses against my jaw.

"Get up and turn around," says Bones.

I can't think of anything else to do, so I rise from Carl's big frame and turn my back to them. Then I spot the chestnut as he starts unrolling his manhood, getting ready to take a nervous pee. At first, it reminds me I need to do the same, then a thought strikes like lightning.

Carl sniffs, trying to stop the blood leaking from his nose. Then he reaches for me, and I put my hands behind me. But as he grabs my left hand and looks at it to snap on the cuff, I drop down, then lurch toward him, slamming a shoulder into his midsection, sending him reeling behind the horses.

Now the gelding has let it all hang out, and he's ready to do his number, but the sudden movement makes him hesitate, and I duck under him and give his crank a yank as I move beneath his belly and out the other side. He lets out a piercing whinny of protest and bucks both hind legs straight back. One of the flashing hooves catches Carl on the side of the head, and there's a crunching thud when his cranium absorbs the blow. He flops face down into a drift.

I stay low, ducking under the second gelding, while scrabbling for the knife strapped to my leg. As I emerge from the other side, I slip the knife out of the scabbard. Bones seems paralyzed, staring down at Carl who's lying on the ground like a heart-shot deer. Then he looks up, sees me, and raises his pistol. I slam the butt of the knife into the bay's flank.

He bucks, but Bones has seen this trick before, and he's a tad smarter than Carl, so he moves to the side to avoid the flailing legs. I pause long enough to throw the knife at Bones, then take off for the ranch house. From the corner of my eye I see Marisol running up behind Bones, and I wonder if she's going to shoot him.

As I charge at top speed toward the house, which is more like a stride, then a skip, I look to see whether my knife brought Bones down, or if Marisol got him. He's cursing, and I see him yank the knife from his left forearm and toss it aside. Probably a painful wound, but not enough to stop him.

Marisol has paused, watching us both. Will groans, but with little force to it.

Bones sights his pistol and fires two quick rounds at me. One of them smacks against the corner of the house, about shoulder high, splintering the wood. The other goes whizzing by my ear, sounding like a hornet in full attack mode.

I reach the house and make the turn, gaining cover, but Bones is storming after me, and he'll soon have the angle to mow me down. The only weapon I have left is my belt buckle knife. Not much help.

I grab open the door, propel myself inside, then slam it shut. But Bones is right behind me, already twisting the door-knob. I cut to the right and charge into my father-in-law's bedroom. And then I see it—hanging on the wall, a gun rack made from horseshoes set into a weathered board. Cradling a worn .30-.30 Winchester. But is it loaded?

I slide across the carpet, bang into the wall and snatch the rifle from its mount. Bones barges inside, spots me, and fires a shot that slams into the wall just inches from my hand. I dodge, whirl around as I work the lever action, and hold the rifle waist high, pointed at his gut. Bones hesitates. I didn't have time to check whether a cartridge chambered into the rifle, so I'm operating under the good graces of the cosmic guardian of firearms.

Bones snarls like a feral wolf and aims his pistol at my heart. I pull the trigger, shooting from the hip. Just as I did with my BB gun a million times as a kid.

There's a loud explosion, and I suck in a breath, waiting for the pain. But I feel nothing, except for the thunderous pounding of my heart. And now I realize I felt the rifle kick.

Bones gets an expression like the amateur actors on the soaps trying for amazement. Eyes wide, mouth open . . . but even better, a finger-sized hole in his lower chest starts leaking blood. His gun drops from his grip, and he tumbles to the floor like a sack of grain.

Marisol walks up behind him, staring down at his fallen form. She's holding her Glock, her hand trembling. "Are you all right, Max?"

"Better off than our two friends. How about you?"

"Panicked, but I'm fine."

"What about Will?"

"We'll have to check."

I start to hang the rifle back on the wall and go give Marisol a hug. But then it hits me that she hasn't holstered up her Glock. I pause and turn my head.

"Put it up. We need to talk." She stresses her remark by hitching the barrel of her Glock.

It's always bad news when a woman says, "We need to talk." It usually means they don't want your sorry self around them anymore. But it's super bad when the gal's got a pistol.

Chapter 30

We go back outside. Carl hasn't moved. Will is still lying there, moaning, so I check him. His pulse is weak, he's sweaty, and he's pale. I pull open his shirt, and the wounds look bad.

He's trying to tell me something. I hand Marisol my phone and tell her to call 9-1-1. I cradle his head with my arm, and he wheezes as he says, "What happened in there?"

"I had to shoot Bones. He's dead. But you just take it easy, and we'll get you an ambulance right away."

"If I don't make it," he says, "can my folks still get the money?"

Marisol folds up the phone, kneels beside us, and says. "Of course, Will. No problem. But we're betting you'll still be spending it on a beach somewhere."

Whoa. What, now? "What do you mean, Marisol?" I ask.

Her forehead wrinkles, her mouth tightens. "I guess you might as well know it all."

My head is spinning, but I try to act receptive. She lets out a long breath, then says, "The bosses in the scheme got worried when Carl and Bones got too active. Their orders were to take out only one of the group, then try to threaten or bribe the others."

"So what happened?"

She fiddles with the zipper on her jacket. "The kid in Denver told them to fuck off, that he was going to call the FBI and the cops. So they used poison gas to take him out when

234

he was jogging—to make it look like a natural death."

"Maybe prussic acid?" I say.

Marisol looks stunned. "That's right, Max. How in the world did you—"

"Doesn't matter. What about the kid in San Francisco? Did someone rig his auto crash?"

"No, that was a pure and simple accident. We were still trying to bargain with the remaining kids as best we could."

"And Will?" I stare at him as I ask. He groans and looks away. I was afraid he would.

"He took our offer to cease and desist and cooperate however possible."

"How much did you pay him?"

"Half a mil."

"Wow. So, Will, would you have shot me to get that money?"

He gives a small shake of his head, then whispers, "No, I'm no killer. I was just trying to save myself and the others."

"I'm sure. And Marisol, what would have happened if Will hadn't taken your offer?"

"Now, Max. Don't get so theatrical. We figured he and the others would be reasonable."

"Ah, yes. Reasonable. That is, they'd do it your way."

She looks weary from the debate. "Whatever. The thing is, it worked out fine, and we just need to go on from here."

"And does that include you and me? How will that work out?"

She looks into my eyes, her face softening. "We'll say that Carl and Bones were hired by some unknown mobster trying to steal the kids' new programs. And we shot them in self-defense." She turns to Will. "You'll go along with that, right?"

He looks sick, but he nods and mumbles, "Yeah, whatever you say."

And now I hear a faint wail of a siren. Probably the sheriff, but it could be the ambulance. Binga would have heard it before now, and I wonder how she's doing. Now Marisol picks up on it. She stiffens, and her eyes widen.

"Max, did you call someone?"

"Yep, the sheriff. But it could be the ambulance."

"No, I didn't call them."

I stare at her in shock.

Will moans, shivers, then slumps in my arms. Panicked, I check his carotid artery. Nothing going on. I lean down by his mouth. He's not breathing.

The siren's louder now, and Marisol moves close to me. I can smell her scented body, along with a musky smell from the action and emotion of the day. "You know I wouldn't have let you get hurt, don't you? That's the reason I came out here. You're the most important person in my life."

Her large coffee eyes absorb my soul and my strength. She's one beautiful woman, not to mention smart, fun, and incredibly sexy. In a low voice, I say, "I don't know if I can trust what you tell me."

She leans against me, and my heart bangs against its walls. *"Corazon,"* she says, "I always cared for you, but that's not the question. You'll just have to trust me. Believe in me, darling. I do love you, and I want you in my life."

The siren sounds very close, and now I hear a car slowing and pulling into the gravel entrance to the ranch. I'll have to make a quick decision. And come up with a plausible story to back it up.

"Kiss me, Marisol. And I hope you'll really mean it."

She does, and my lips melt against hers, our hot tongues exploring, our bodies melding, one into the other. God, she feels good. But is this for real?

As the car approaches, we disengage. Marisol gives me a

last, soulful glance. The sheriff's car stops, and he and Travis emerge. They don't draw their weapons, but I can see they're keeping their gun hands real close to the iron. And they're checking out the scene with wary cops' eyes.

"What's going on, Max?"

The sheriff and I go back a long ways. I've never lied to him before, and he knows it. Besides, we both believe in truth and justice.

"It's a long story, Frank. First, thanks for coming. We're okay, now, so let's sit down and let me fill you in."

The lawmen relax a bit, but they're still mighty curious. They're taking in Carl's body stretched out on the ground, one side of his head crushed. And Will, lying there dead, with gunshot wounds in the chest. They haven't even seen Bones sprawled on the floor in the house.

Frank keys the mike on his shirt, saying, "This is Frank. We need an evidence team at the Rocking Six Ranch on Aiken Switch road. And make it quick."

We move into the lower section of the house and sit down. I introduce Marisol. Then I say, "It all started when I got a call that Detective Bagley's son was in trouble." I describe the murders, mention the accident in San Francisco, and fill them in about the dead hit men and Will.

Marisol listens intently, as tense as a barn swallow watching a prowling cat. But I manage to leave her failings and human weaknesses out of the story. And with the troubles the FBI has had lately, I can't bring myself to sling any mud at them.

"So, that's the short version, Hank," I say. Well, it's one version, at least.

The sheriff and undersheriff look stunned. Hank takes a look at the bodies on the ground, clears his throat, and says, "Travis, tape off the scene. We'll get their full statements later." As Travis moves off, Hank scrutinizes me and Marisol for a long second, then says, "You got a complicated tale there, Max. Better make sure those two statements jibe."

"No problem, Sheriff."

As he turns to begin his gory job, I fix Marisol with a look. "You know what I want you to do, don't you?"

"Resign from the Bureau?" Her eyes tear up, and her lower lip starts to quiver.

I hug her to me, comforting both her and myself. Then I raise her chin to study those luminous eyes. "No, Marisol. I think you're a helluva agent. You got in a tight situation with no good solution. But this crap stops now, or I'll see to it the whole country finds out."

"What should I—"

"Call John now, tell him to ditch the program and go back to doing the job the right way. And tell him to not even think about coming after me. I'll have the information squirreled away in several safe places before he can get someone here."

She seems to shrink a bit, but she pulls out her phone and makes the call. Her voice wavers as she talks, but she seems to get no argument from her boss. We'll see what happens.

After Marisol and I give our statements to the sheriff, I call the vet's office. Binga is sleeping, her vital signs good. They say I can pick her up tomorrow. Her leg will be stiff and sore for a couple of weeks, they tell me, but then she should be fine. I'm relieved, feeling some tension ease away.

Marisol and I leave the ranch, heading east on Highway 70 toward Kansas City, where I'll drop her off for her flight back home. We're not talking, and I have time to think about what happened, and what might be in the future for everyone involved. I'll contact Damian Roberts's parents in San Francisco to let them know the car wreck was an accident, and I'll also inform Jennifer's mom in Denver that, partly thanks to

Jennifer's alertness, we were able to catch the bad guys. As for me, I'll go back to stargazing and yoga and nature walks. But what of my nonexistent love life?

I do care for Marisol. Deeply and for all time? I don't know. And I'm too skeptical of Lieutenant Bartles in Denver to entertain further romantic ideas about her. Basically, I'm back to square one in the relationship department. So what's new?

Except that I do harbor strong feelings for Amy Harrington. I've just been so busy with this case that I couldn't call her. Or maybe I thought that the tug I felt toward Marisol might develop into something real and lasting. It's hard to learn so late in your life that relationships and institutional choices and the honor and integrity of man are all so fragile and shaky.

"There's nothing new under the Sun," someone once said. But maybe we could become more decent human beings if we would be conscious of the stars, count our blessings, and value the special gift of existence we've received.

As Henry Van Dyke wrote, we should all "Be thankful for life! Because it gives you the chance to love and to work, to play and to look up at the stars."

So when I get home, I'll drink a beer, spend a while staring at planets and stars, then gratefully hit the hay. Tomorrow, I'll pick up Binga and bring her back to resume our pleasant and peaceful country life. Before long, I'll even get back into investigating the evil that men do.

That is, if some sneaky asteroid or comet doesn't take dead aim at our planet. But that's in the hands of fate. Or destiny. Or the will of God. But hasn't it always been that way?

About the Author

Mark Bouton majored in sociology at Oklahoma State University and earned a law degree at the Oklahoma University School of Law. He entered the FBI, and for 30 years worked cases in Mobile, Alabama; New York; Chicago; Puerto Rico; Brownsville, Texas; San Antonio; and Topeka, Kansas. During his career, he captured killers, kidnappers, con men, bank robbers, and terrorists. He worked many high-profile cases, including playing a key role in solving the Oklahoma City bombing. Father of four sons, he lives in Kansas, where he writes novels, lifts weights and practices yoga. He also often contemplates the universe. He's currently writing two mystery series. For more information, visit his Web site at http://www.markbouton.com.

2006 Oct.
$25.95